THE AMERICAN SPELLBOUND

BY KATYA G. COHEN

Berwick Court Publishing Co.
Chicago, IL

Although this story was inspired by the author's real life story, characters and events are not intended to represent specific people or events.

Berwick Court Publishing Company
Chicago, Illinois
http://www.berwickcourt.com

Cohen, Katya G.
  The American spellbound / by Katya G. Cohen.

  pages ; cm

  Issued also as an ebook.
  ISBN: 978-0-9889540-8-3

  1. Women stockbrokers--United States--Fiction. 2. Floor traders (Finance)--United States--Fiction. 3. Financial crises--United States. 4. Stocks--Moral and ethical aspects. 5. Russian Americans--Fiction. 6. Wall Street (New York, N.Y.)--Fiction. I. Title.

PS3603.O44 A44 2014
813/.6   2014954428

BERNARD: *But sometimes, Willy, it's better for a man just to walk away.*

WILLY: *Walk away?*

BERNARD: *That's right.*

WILLY: *But if you can't walk away?*

BERNARD: *I guess that's when it's tough.*

– Arthur Miller, *Death of a Salesman*

Chapter

1

VIKA STAKHANOVA SAT IN HER bathroom reading *Departures* magazine. It was 6:15 a.m. She had been reading the same page of the magazine for a few weeks now. She was trying to read it, but all she did was stare at the sentences while her mind wandered off. "Are you still showering with ordinary municipal water? That's so old school!" the article began, listing the benefits of installing a vitamin C-infused shower in your bathroom. The over-the-top luxurious lifestyle featured in all seriousness in the magazine carried an entertainment value for Vika, and she read it for laughs, to behold the creative depravity of high-end living. Besides, the magazine came free with her American Express platinum card.

Vika wasn't laughing, however. As a mid-level employee

at a proprietary desk at Royal Oakleys Bank PLC, a large British bank, she was worrying about the choppy bond market and unexpected moves by the government, all of which could affect her year-end bonus in a bad way. She was on a losing streak and was trying to get her money back. Vika had to be at her desk by 7 a.m. All bond trading, the kind that matters anyway, wraps up by 8:30 a.m., an hour before the stock market even opens. Yesterday, she was 2 points above water on her $15 million position in a synthetic bond index, but any sudden move would wipe out that thin advantage. Several times in the past few weeks, she was in the money but failed to take the profits off, only to end up with yet another loss. She had to hurry up and get to work, but, in a spell of morning lethargy, she kept reading the same sentences over and over.

Vika worked in Midtown Manhattan. The commute from her Village apartment only took about fifteen minutes by subway, door to door. Instead, she preferred to take an eight-minute taxi ride to her office, as the quiet solitude of the back of a cab enabled her to get to work undisturbed. She loathed being distracted from her morning meditations by the subway masses. Even more annoying than the commuting rubes was the act of waiting for a train, even for two minutes. The wait, the idleness, had a suffocating effect on Vika. Her Blackberry didn't have a signal underground and she didn't want to be disconnected from the world, even for a minute. When there's possible early morning action in the bond market, you want to be present and participating. For Vika, being stuck on the subway train meant that someone else, not her, was learning the news the moment it came out, that someone else was making money out there. The fear of missing out was too excruciating to use public transit.

So far, 2009 hadn't been a good year for Vika. A great move down that she profitably rode all the way to the bottom the year before gave way to a choppy, volatile market. Her last few trades were abysmal. Even when she was in the money, the market's sudden and violent mood swings prevented her from cashing in. She wistfully remembered the high she felt during the last year's carnage, when everything moved only one way — down. Being in the money on her trades awarded her a certain superiority. She felt like she had earned the right to mock others' trade ideas and interrupt them at meetings and dismiss their arguments. Being down on her trades would turn her into the desk pariah. Losing made Vika feel *emasculated*.

But it wasn't the prospect of losing money that gave Vika the biggest chills, it was the possibility of losing future action. Losing the access to action makes you impotent, empty of promise. For a trader — hell, for any American — being empty of promise is an abomination. There is a reason "What do you do?" has replaced all other forms of greeting on this side of the Atlantic. Lack of action meant sitting and waiting for something to happen, not being able to go out and get it for herself. Without access to action, she would be just an average wage slave at the mercy of others. She would have to pretend, to be nice to assholes, servile to superiors; she'd have to behave. She couldn't speak her mind and she'd have to nod in agreement while listening to others' bullshit.

But having access to the "book,"[1] to the "P&L," awarded her special powers. It is all about the next trade, the next

---

1 The amount of money a trader or portfolio manager has at his disposal.

spin of the wheel; you're always just a few spins away from hitting the jackpot. Whoever stands between you and that magic lever is denying you a chance at a better tomorrow. Coming between a trader and his book is like coming between a blue-haired old lady and her lucky slot machine: You will be denying them their *pursuit of happiness*.

Vika was afraid that her boss was on the verge of halting her trading, of perhaps even taking away her book. That prospect was so terrifying for Vika that the thought always gave her cold sweats and a knot in her stomach. Vika knew that a few more missteps, a few more losses, and this would all be over. If she couldn't make money on her trades, she'd be condemned to a bleak future. And she was prepared to fight the possibility of that separation with the determination of a junkie. It's all just a temporary setback. The next trade will be a sure winner. She just has to listen to Street chatter, pick good entry points and be more disciplined in taking off profits.

On Wall Street, you don't let temporary setbacks stop you. You don't retreat into a hole — you get up, dust yourself off and, like Sisyphus, continue on your path. Even if you don't succeed, the whole point is to be on the upward slope; the motion itself gives you purpose. What kind of purpose? Who cares, as long as it keeps you busy and well-paid! It's the American Way.

That evening, Vika was scheduled to go to a charity event. The event, organized by the Big Dreams We Deliver Foundation — one of the biggest New York charities — attracted most of the Wall Street and hedge fund charity-circuit crowd. The foundation's sole focus was doling out merit scholarships to underprivileged New York children. For any self-respecting New York charity, it's important to attach itself to kids from the ghetto. "It's for the children" is a subtle middle finger to any skeptic who doubts the movers and shakers' benevolent impulse. For the bet-making crowd, charity is a cheap option: For an annual donation that will hardly make a dent in your wallet, your personal brand becomes immune to criticism and is preserved for posterity. Plus you get to hang out with various celebrities and star athletes.

The annual black-tie gala took place at Cipriani 42nd Street. The venue, rivaling the size of the majestic train station across the street, used to host a bank once, back in the days when banks sought to project prudence and stability. Today, the monumental architecture of the ballroom, the massive marble columns, the seventy-foot ceilings adorned with golden chandeliers, and the fawning white-gloved personnel provided an appropriate setting for the usual assortment of New York egos, each as big as a freight train. But, for all the opulence and the important crowd and the braised lamb shanks, Vika knew she wasn't going to enjoy it. The only thing she welcomed about such events was the excuse to dress up. She already got herself a chic, abstractly patterned, yellow-green Marni dress that would make her stand out from the sea of all those ubiquitous, bourgeois little black dresses. But she dreaded the conversations and the mindless mingling and the standard icebreakers of "What do you do?" and "How big is your P&L?"

Vika couldn't explain why she kept going to these events though. Despite her previous lackluster experience, she still expected more excitement and adventure from these black-tie gatherings than they actually delivered. Instead of working on her social skills, Vika had perfected the skill of drinking alone over the years. As someone who considered herself a realist, Vika resented pretense and usually resigned herself to people-watching.

"…Democrats are going to throw so much money at the problem, we will be bankrupt in a year!" She heard a middle-aged guy in an ill-fitting suit, instead of a tuxedo, engaging a group of women in their 20s in tight dresses and those hideous platform Louboutins. "I'll be stocking up on canned beans and moving to a shack in the woods." Vika recognized Lenny Lucferovsky, her headhunter. Any political talk, especially from a Russian, had an unhinging effect on Vika, so she decided to break her solitude and, with a determined look, approached the group.

"First of all, it was the free-market, leave-us-alone Republicans who started throwing money at the problem a year ago. Second, it's hard for me to picture you living in the woods."

The flock of young women, as if waiting for an excuse to escape the boring blather of an old man, used this intrusion to disperse.

"Vika, dear, why do you have to be so aggressive? You have to hide your Kalashnikov[2] when you talk to people, you scare them off." Lenny sounded annoyed. "People are here to have a good time and you have to come in and ruin it with your politics."

"Oh, excuse me. Did I ruin your attempts to get laid?"

---

2   Russian-made AK-47 machine gun.

Vika grinned.

"Maybe you did. I have to take every chance I can before, one day, I won't be able to get it up."

"You mean you still can? What are you, 52, 53?"

"Bitch."

They both giggled.

"Look at all these fucks," Vika said, gazing over the room with derision. "Do you really think they are here for the charity?"

"Vika, they are not fucks, they are my customers. And I can't believe that you think that this has anything to do with charity."

"They can be your customers and still be fucks."

"Sweetheart, have you considered that the reason you dislike them so much is because you're one of them? And you can't be anything else. And it bugs you."

Before Vika could tell Lenny to go fuck himself, he was gone, distracted by yet another potential client.

Vika was one of them. But over the years, she had built a thick enough mental shield to block the unpleasant thoughts.

"Hey, Vika," she heard someone say. She turned around. "How's it going?" Some guy she had certainly met before was approaching her. "What are you doing these days?" Vika recognized him as an old colleague, the guy she used to sit opposite while she was a low-level employee at Baruch Wolf years ago. An acquaintance really, not even a buddy. He was well dressed, with fake cheer on his face.

"Hey, how are you… Kevin?" She took a few seconds

to remember his name. "So, where are you now?" Vika asked a standard question in a standard situation.

"Well, since Baruch collapsed, I've been in a free fall. Looking for a job now," he said and smiled. He never smiled when they worked together at Baruch Wolf, Vika thought.

"Isn't it nice to have a year off?" Vika said reflectively.

"Well, yeah, sure it's nice, but I'd like to have a job now," he answered, not inclined to chit-chat.

Vika knew that he had a family to support and she felt sorry for him. But she couldn't help him.

"Here's my card," she said. "Just shoot me a Bloomberg.[3] If I hear anything, I'll let you know."

"Thanks. I don't have Bloomberg these days, so I'll shoot you an email."

"Sure, no prob."

He put Vika's business card in his pocket and slumped away to another group of people.

"He paid $750 to come here and mingle and humiliate himself like this," Vika thought bleakly. "Is this what's in store for all of us here?"

After the dinner and the feel-good, self-congratulatory speeches from Wall Street bigwigs, and the parade of a few lucky scholarship recipients on stage, Vika walked out of Cipriani, took a deep breath, and proceeded toward a taxi stand.

Near the Grand Central entrance, she saw a bum. He wasn't a usual bum. He was a man in his late 50s to early 60s in a cheap but neatly maintained business suit, a former

---

3   Bloomberg trading terminal instant message.

accountant perhaps, or a bank teller. He held an "I ♥ NY" plastic bag in one hand and a cardboard sign in the other. Vika never gave money to bums on subways or on the street, as she thought they were mostly faking it. But there was too much discomfort about this man. It was obvious he wasn't standing there on a whim. He looked embarrassed as he hid his gaze away from an approaching Vika. "Laid off after 20 years on the job. Have a family to feed," read his cardboard sign. This didn't seem like the usual case of hustling. Vika, in high heels, didn't want to cross the street to avoid passing him, so she approached him.

"Uh, are you hungry or something?" Vika didn't find anything better to say and felt slightly embarrassed by her opening line.

"Well, someone gave me a sandwich here," the man replied, lifting a hand with a plastic bag.

"Uh, don't you get unemployment or something?"

"I ran out, it's been more than a year," he said apologetically.

"Here, take it." Vika pulled a $20 bill out of her purse gave it to the man without making eye contact and quickly walked away, looking sideways to make sure no one had seen her.

"If I don't make money soon, I'll be that guy," she thought.

Chapter 2

VIKA WAS BORN IN 1974 on the outskirts of Moscow in a gray, dull industrial town with one of those witless, insipid names that Soviet-era bureaucrats bestowed indiscriminately across the country, running out of names of Great Russian writers, painters and scientists by the time the town was due for renaming. Her father died of a heart attack when she was 5 and her mother succumbed to cancer ten years later. Due to the bureaucratic chaos of the crumbling state — and thanks to a few envelopes strategically handed to government officials by her older sister — Vika, though a minor, was allowed to continue to live in her late mother's apartment. State officials appointed Vika's sister, who was married and lived nearby with her husband, to be her legal guardian.

Vika's future prospects were a widely discussed topic

for neighbors and townsfolk, who drew their own conclusions about a teenage girl living alone. Vika, unaware of the public bets made at her expense, disappointed them in their gloomy forecasts; she simply immersed herself in her studies as a way of coping with her mother's death. Perhaps intentionally, her mother made the process easier. Before her death, sensing the end but hiding it from Vika, she became irascible and rude — an odd reversal from her usually cheerful and good-natured disposition. This sudden change, Vika later explained to herself, happened because "mother wanted to hurt me so I wouldn't grieve as much when she was gone."

While scarred by the death of a parent, as any child would be, Vika discovered that her mother's death awarded her special advantages and liberated her from the usual teenage plagues like curfews and constant parental control. Her loss became the envy of every local teenager: Live alone in your own apartment, do whatever the hell you want — how cool is that? And yet, such sudden liberation came with the realization that, unlike her peers, defiant and rebellious against authority, Vika had no one to rebel against. She was free to do as she chose. The weight of this revelation gave her pause.

As a result of this newfound awareness, Vika's life was rather boring given the circumstances: Drunken parties did happen at her place at the insistence of her classmates, but it was others who got into trouble, not her. She found the role of an observer much more satisfying than that of a participant. After graduating high school with excellent grades, Vika didn't particularly want to enroll in college. Fed up with constant poverty, she expressed an interest in working at an ice cream kiosk at the Leningradsky railway station, where she had worked the previous summer and was able to amass a 300-ruble fortune, which she used to buy a pair of jeans and a two-week trip to Crimea. Her older sister, horrified by her choice of profession, grabbed Vika and her high school diploma and dragged her to the admissions office of the top economics school in Moscow: Plekhanov Moscow Institute of the National Economy. Vika passed the entry exams, but just barely, as the entry system into the prestigious Plekhanov Institute was notoriously rigged to make room for the children of the well connected.

Her college years were tough, not in an academic sense, but because of the alienation she felt surrounded by the rich offspring of party officials and the emerging class of the nouveaux riches. Money shortage was a persistent drag on her self-esteem. Her meager stipend — her only source of income — prevented her from joining others for lunch in the cafeteria. She also skipped parties because she didn't want to be the worst-dressed person in the room. The only way she could make friends with any of her classmates was by lending them her lecture notes, as they never bothered to show up to the lectures. As the economic crisis of the early '90s abated, things became easier. One could get part-time employment, which Vika promptly did at a travel agency. Her English was particularly good, as, since about the age of 12, she'd nurtured a dream to get out of that "goddamn place" by whatever means, and gave English special attention and care in high school and college.

Employment, even part-time, provided some relief and an opportunity to practice English with native speakers.

Four years passed by and, after graduating in 1995, Vika landed an entry-level job at Citibank, which had just opened an office in Moscow. Citi–freaking-bank, she thought — the subject of case studies in college, the topic of articles she read in *The Economist*, an almost mythical organization, one of the biggest banks in the world. Finally, she was earning a good salary of $800 a month but, accustomed to an ascetic lifestyle, was saving most of it. Vika was never as close to realizing her dream as she was now and she wasn't going to screw it up. It was time to begin considering a big jump to the place that, until now, existed only in distant dreams and in movies — *the U. S. of A.*

Vika discarded the idea of going to the U.S. as a tourist and staying there illegally afterward, as many did in those days. Instead, she decided to apply to a number of graduate schools and get a student visa. The school's rank was the least of her concerns, she only cared if she could afford the first semester or two, as she could not get any sort of outside financial help or apply for any student loans. She saved up around $4,000 and found a school, Arizona Baptist University, which cost $2,100 a semester. The word "Baptist" in the name of the school made her a little uncomfortable, but she figured she could just ignore those pesky "Jesus freaks" — a new term she learned from a chuckling American acquaintance in Moscow when she revealed her destination to him.

"You? Phoenix? Baptist University? Ha ha ha! Please, send me regular updates," he bantered. Vika wasn't amused. After all, focusing on her studies and blocking out noise was her specialty. The GMAT turned out to be a difficult test for her, as American tests do not favor the contemplative disposition she tried to apply to a time-sensitive exercise. Her math scores saved her.

Vika arrived in Phoenix in January of 1997.

Arizona Baptist University, a Southern Baptist school in west Phoenix — a decrepit area surrounded by low-income neighborhoods, dollar stores, pawnshops and auto repair shops — was an odd match for an ambitious spirit from Moscow. The two main contingents of ABU were local entrepreneurs looking for business degrees to run their own companies, and rowdy, ADD-prone children of local small-business owners who put them into the religious school, all expenses paid, in the hopes they would "get religion."

Vika now understood what so entertained her American friend back in Moscow about the idea of her going to Phoenix. "But what the hell was I supposed to do? It was either this or stay in Moscow," she would counsel herself. To her relief, no one tried to actively convert her: Southern Baptists were a bit more civilized than the well-known proselytizers, like Moonies or Jehovah's Witnesses, although she received plenty of friendly invitations for "Church on Sunday." But she'd discovered a low tolerance for religious talk from people who had never heard of Nietzsche and had never traveled farther than fifty miles from Phoenix. Such close-mindedness rubbed her the wrong way.

At first, Vika engaged her roommates in passionate debates about religion, but soon realized it was a hopeless endeavor. She discovered that the evangelicals were the ones who "didn't want to find out," who already had answers to everything, so whatever argument she made, however logical, fell on deaf ears. So, after a while, she abandoned this exercise in futility. Astonished and somewhat depressed by this mentality that permeated the campus residents, Vika welcomed any friendships with the non-religious — mostly Asian and European students who perhaps ended up at ABU due to circumstances similar to hers.

***

As her savings began to evaporate, Vika, for a few months, took up a part-time janitor job on campus for $5 an hour — a fact that was subsequently kept secret from even her closest friends and family. While working as a janitor, Vika became acquainted with a strange category of people whom she found more interesting and genuine than the campus Jesus freaks. They were white, worked low-wage jobs or subsisted on some unknown resources, not entirely religious — at least, they didn't bother going to church or talking about it — smoked weed and, she suspected, something much stronger. But they were instantly friendly, entertaining and most importantly, unlike evangelicals, they appeared non-judgmental.

The poor whites intrigued Vika. These folks lived their lives as if they were driving their battered Camaros into the sunset with a Bon Jovi ballad playing in the background. Vika, always looking for ways to explain things, attributed such resignation to their innate philosophical understanding of life. The poor Russians she knew back home, alcoholics and degenerates though they were, could quote all the major classicists and philosophers. Why shouldn't she attribute these same qualities to poor Americans? Poverty and a depraved social status did not have to translate into lack of wits in her book. She even tried to discuss Carlos Castaneda's books with them: You know, American Southwest, desert, peyote-induced hallucinations — surely, they must be able to relate. She didn't get far with it though.

Charm is a potent weapon of the destitute and aimless person, most effective when directed at an uninitiated newcomer. When Vika's car, a 13-year-old Nissan Sentra, refused to start one day, one of her co-workers told her to talk to Jimmy Ray, a fellow "custodian."

"Are you Jimmy Ray?" Vika approached a guy who was taking a smoke break in 100-degree heat in the parking lot outside the student center.

"Who wants to know?" he answered, sizing her up, grinning, eager at a chance to demonstrate his wit to some new girl, a foreign girl!

Jimmy Ray Turner, 32 years young, who carried his pack of Kamel Reds rolled up in his T-shirt sleeve on the shoulder exposing a tattoo of a naked big-breasted woman, knew when to be charming. His standard uniform of jeans, a T-shirt and an occasional plaid shirt with cutoff sleeves, combined with a lifelong disregard for sunscreen under the Phoenix sun, gave Jimmy Ray a quintessential American Southern Boy look, although he'd never been to the real South. Born in California, he moved to Phoenix with his mother as a child, where she died of cancer when Jimmy Ray was in his early 20s. Jimmy Ray and Vika bonded over this fact.

For Vika, Jimmy Ray was a local curiosity, a type she had never met before and she welcomed their friendship. Her curiosity was almost anthropological, as one would observe a tribesman in his natural habitat. She absorbed the white-trash culture that he oozed, his taste in music, the American trivia, the idioms and the mentality. Vika never worried, however, about slipping into that way of life for real — she was an observer temporarily living among her study subjects. Besides, for the time being, she couldn't afford to have a different circle of friends.

For the powerless, there's always a story — always a smoothly constructed narrative that explains their misfortunes. The abandon and fatalism with which Jimmy Ray treated matters of importance puzzled Vika. Jimmy Ray had never finished college, although, as he told Vika, he took some accounting classes at some now-defunct for-profit college, for which he took out a $3,000 student loan. After that school shut down due to mismanagement, Jimmy Ray couldn't repay the loan and, with this debt still outstanding, couldn't get a new one to finish up the degree at a different school. Thus, he reasoned, he was stuck in limbo due to circumstances beyond his control. Vika thought that such defeatism in the face of a mere $3,000 hole was odd when measured against a lifetime of low-paying jobs. Jimmy Ray compensated such resignation toward vital matters by being defiant and passionate about things that had no impact on his life.

"Bullshiet! Bullshiet!" Jimmy Ray, sitting in his La-Z-Boy chair with a bottle of Old Milwaukee in hand, would scream at TV screen where Bill Clinton was defending himself against the investigative committee. Vika, genuinely dumbfounded about why this was a big deal, got her first taste of the American moralistic obsession with sex and politics, and of the deliberate self-sabotage of the destitute. Jimmy Ray was her medium to this ugly but fascinating side of American life, and Vika couldn't help but watch in awe.

Soon, Vika got a data-entry job, open to foreign students as a part-time, paid internship, at the Arizona State Retirement System. It paid $10 an hour and Vika, somehow convincing the Human Resources department to let her work full time, was able to breathe more easily about her finances. Jimmy Ray got a job at a local head shop. Eager to get off the dreaded campus, she and Jimmy Ray rented an apartment together on West Osborn Road. Vika had to put her name on the lease because Jimmy Ray could not get approved with his abysmal credit history. Vika didn't have much of a credit history, not yet anyway, but it was still better than Jimmy Ray's.

After a few months, Jimmy Ray couldn't pay his share of rent. He supplied a multitude of excuses: His boss was a jerk and he had to quit; he got robbed at gunpoint (he couldn't go to the police because of an equally abysmal legal history); he had to lend $200 to his friend Matt as a down payment for a carpet cleaning business they were going to start together. He always had a story.

One time, Vika got home from school and didn't find a desktop computer they had purchased together on credit (under her name, of course). To her further outrage, her treasured Led Zeppelin IV album was also gone. Jimmy Ray had taken it all to the pawnshop because he needed money to repair his car to get to work, but swore he was going to get it back the next day. "Money is coming in soon," he would say. "You're my princess and I'll take care of you."

Vika cringed at the thought and at the use of such wretched language. "Princess? What the hell?" Vika thought. She started a paper spreadsheet that she kept under a magnet on the refrigerator to keep track of Jimmy Ray's monetary shortfalls. The figure soon got into the thousands. One day, the spreadsheet disappeared and a love note appeared on the kitchen counter. Vika, patient up to a point, got the message, but not the one Jimmy Ray had intended. She became enraged. With graduation on the horizon, she went to a travel agency and purchased the cheapest one-way ticket to New York. Having a ticket with a set date on which she was to leave Phoenix, most likely forever, gave her mental relief.

She wasn't yet familiar with the concept of cutting her losses, but she was certain that her Phoenix affair had to end as quickly as possible. Poor Jimmy Ray was shocked when he found out. Vika expected an angry fit, but when the realization sunk in that she wasn't bluffing, Jimmy Ray started weeping and pleading. He desperately pushed buttons that had worked on every woman in his past, but failed to have any effect on Vika.

"But I love you! How can you be so cruel?" he begged.

Vika almost cried, too, at the sight of such indignity, of a grown man weeping. She almost felt sorry for the guy. What if he really loved her? But then it dawned on her:

"No. You love yourself *with me*," she countered.

Jimmy Ray stopped crying and processed what she had just said, slowly grasping that his love card had been trumped.

He made another attempt for her sympathy. "You're killing me."

"You're dragging me down!" she shot back. "I'm sorry, but I can't stay in Phoenix. I gotta leave."

She was incredulous and angry, mostly with herself for having pitied this guy. "Does he really think we have a future together?" she wondered. "How stupid does he think I am? How stupid am I?"

"I'll leave you my car," she said. "I'll change the title to your name tomorrow." She figured she couldn't possibly sell that piece of junk and Jimmy Ray could definitely use a set of wheels.

"How is it even possible to be that delusional?" she marveled at Jimmy Ray. "How much energy they spend building their own illusions, only to become trapped in them."

Chapter
3

Vika took a gamble moving to New York. She would stay in the basement of an old Moscow friend who lived in West Babylon on Long Island and look for a job. She had a clear plan: If she didn't find a job within a month or two, she would go back to Moscow. Not that she wanted to go back. But not having proper documentation, if she somehow failed to change her immigration status from a student to an employee, was against her internal rules. Being illegal, she figured, would condemn her to a lifetime of menial labor and this thought depressed her. So her plan was to either find a real job as quickly as possible or return to Moscow and try again later.

Vika's self-esteem suffered a crushing blow after she moved to New York. It turned out she wasn't as well-read as she thought she was. Everyone talked about things and quoted authors she had never heard of. Her degree from Arizona Baptist University, she soon found out, was better left unmentioned during small talk with new acquaintances. People would pause, say "Oh," and give her a pitiful look.

As luck would have it, Vika got a job offer from a medium-sized German bank, SudDeutsche Landesbank, within three weeks of arriving in New York. She was hired in a risk-management unit to help run mortgage-bond analytics. The new employer also sponsored Vika for an H-1B work visa — the most important aspect of the job offer. Like any quasi-governmental German bank, implicitly backed by the full faith and credit of the German government, SudDeutsche Landesbank was a quiet, lethargic institution. Its triple-A rating allowed SudDeutsche to forgo the hustles that any other, lower-rated bank had to engage in to fund itself. The pay at the bank reflected its lackluster business model. Even the front-desk employees weren't paid as much as they would have been at a lower-tiered bank. But what they got instead was peace of mind, stability, and invitations to endless conferences and lavish Christmas parties at prime New York spots.

German Landesbanks had a perfect business model: They borrowed at very low interest rates, relying on their rock-solid credit, and then had the entire yield-producing Wall Street horde knocking on their door. As a prime buy-side client, Landesbank didn't suffer from a lack of wily schmoozers peddling their high-yielding financial products. The portfolio on which Vika ran her analysis consisted mostly of mortgage-backed securities. While Vika wasn't entirely unschooled in bond math, her business-school knowledge of bonds didn't extend beyond the cursory concepts of price/yield relationships and basic cash-flow analysis. But these mortgage bonds were a different breed; unlike plain Treasury bonds, they had risks that were hard to measure, like prepayments and defaults, in addition to interest rate risk. Thousands of math and physics PhDs labored day and night at the desks of Midtown Manhattan office buildings, crunching the entire Greek-alphabet soup of abstruse concepts, trying to gauge the risk of owning such bonds. But the complexity and the associated risk were secondary concerns: Who cares about complexity if it means a 20 percent yield? SudDeutsche Landesbank wanted that yield.

For Vika, even with her low-by-Manhattan-standards pay, this job was still a blessing. Finally, for the first time since moving to the U.S., she could afford to rent her own apartment and, with her modest habits, even save a little. All the survivalist battles that she was fighting just weeks ago suddenly disappeared. Constant worries were cured by a stable paycheck, a legit immigration status, a place of her own. Her workday usually ended around 5:30 p.m., when all the German management headed to nearby pubs. Life was, at last, good.

***

Headhunter Lenny Lucferovsky called Vika and didn't mince words: "You have an interview tomorrow at Baruch Wolf at 9 a.m. Go to the seventh floor and ask for Tom Bryant. Be on time."

"Wait, wait," Vika said. "What kind of job is this?"

"Like the fuck you care, sweetheart." Lenny got quickly

annoyed. "They need bodies and you look like a fit. Just don't fuck it up, detochka."[4] He hung up.

Lenny Lucferovsky was a Russian émigré who came to New York during the third wave of Jewish immigration in the late 1980s. A hustler and a gambler back in the Soviet Union, Lenny went through the usual professional route of a Russian Jew math whiz in New York: NYU Stern School of Business, then a quant job on the trading desk at a major investment bank. However, Lenny, who had a low tolerance for stupid — and that pretty much included everybody in his world — didn't last long on the desk. He quit in a fit of rage at the imbecility of his superiors, thus ending his Wall Street career. For a few years, he made his living playing bridge tournaments and building his own headhunting agency. Occasionally, Lenny made his way down to Atlantic City where, pretending to be slightly retarded, limping and drooling, he crashed high-stakes poker games. It was a good gig while it lasted. His bridge connections landed him his biggest client, Baruch Wolf, as its entire senior management were bridge aficionados.

Baruch Wolf, the smallest of the "bulge bracket" investments banks, was the fiercest, most leveraged and most aggressive among its peers, especially in the mortgage business. Although a publicly traded company, it still maintained a management core reminiscent of an old partnership. Once you started at Baruch, you stayed at Baruch. The senior management was heavily paid in Baruch's stock, large chunks of which were deferred. That sent a strong message to potential traitors: Leave and lose half of your net worth. Such brotherhood, such an "us vs. them" mentality, was nurtured and

4   Russian: little girl, with slightly derisive connotations.

praised at the firm. Management celebrated the "pull oneself up by the bootstraps" background of its hires. Unlike "white shoe" firms — a term always said with derision and sneer within its walls — Baruch Wolf praised itself for being gritty, down to earth and always giving preference to "a poor and hungry kid from Brooklyn who just wants to get rich." Such a selection process over the years turned Baruch Wolf into a predominantly Jewish-Italian shop, and the firm itself was seen on the Street as the young kid with a chip on his shoulder. For Vika, with her own chip on her shoulder and third-tier credentials, a job at Baruch Wolf was a rare chance to get into the big boys' world.

Vika, thanks to an obsessive lifelong habit of always being on time, made sure to arrive at Baruch's Midtown headquarters at 8:45 a.m. and took a few laps around the block to kill time. At 9 a.m. sharp, she was at the seventh floor reception desk and asked for Tom Bryant. "This way," the secretary said, ushering Vika to one of the empty conference rooms.

The interview took about fifteen minutes and she thought it went well. Tom came in with a jaded and weary look, asked her what "duration"[5] meant, where she wanted to be in five years, described to her what they were doing and that was it. She didn't "shit her pants," heeding Lenny's advice. She started at Baruch a week later.

Vika welcomed the rigors of working for a firm like Baruch Wolf. Being at her desk early in the morning and leaving well past midnight, though physically and mentally draining, gave her a sense of purpose. This kind of hard

---

5   A measure of a bond's price sensitivity to a change in interest rates.

work, unlike the hard work she had done before, paid well and provided an opportunity to make a good life, to perhaps even retire early. "If it is a meritocracy, as they say, then I certainly deserve to be here," she thought.

The notion of "hard work" occupies a cult-like status in the minds of both proud Americans and striving immigrants. Hard work brings meaning to our repetitive daily motions. It is revered and sought after. To be a respected member of the American community, you have to be constantly on the move. The "busyness" itself is even more important than the final product. The social utility of that busyness can always be attached later on with skillful narrative and good PR. And no one can sell such a narrative better than the financial industry. They are the providers of liquidity, the market makers, the allocators of capital, the sponsors of small enterprise. They make the economy work. Without them there would be no jobs for anyone else, no capital raised, no credit extended. Therefore, the *more* they work, the *better* the economy works.

Doctors, firefighters and teachers can't create more work for themselves when they are faced with a quiet day, and on such days, they are at peace. Wall Street warriors can't sit idle if things are suddenly quiet. Calm is a four-letter word. Sloth is the biggest sin on the floors and desks of Wall Street. Quiet time carries a risk of being exposed as a mere paper-shuffler, an accountant after tax season, a general during peace time. And Wall Street fights off quiet with all the creativity, smarts and energy it has. Quiet will be disturbed with intentional action, with making something out of nothing, lest some nosy journalist on a mission exposes banking as no different from all other human vocations, just one of many, no worse, no better. No, Wall Street is special, a superior breed; they didn't spend all those years fiddling with spreadsheets and staring at screens for nothing. They have acquired the power that no other industry possesses: Unlike doctors and firefighters, the forward-looking financial industry, with its inherent ingenuity and innovation, can accelerate its contribution to society. And if some know-nothing ingrate complains, just show him how many people were able to buy homes in the past few years. Say whatever you want, but making all that happen, that's hard work.

Vika didn't bother herself with such thoughts. Finally able to afford a nice, middle-class life in the big city, and with memories of hardship still fresh, she worked for good pay and a possible promotion; she had no time to ruminate on the virtues of Wall Street.

Vika's group was responsible for "cracking mortgage collateral tapes," to use Wall Street lingo. This job involved organizing loan-level information received from mortgage lenders across the country into easy-to-read summary tables. Then those tables were passed on to traders and structurers who could bid on the loan portfolio, buy the loans, structure the deal and market it to clients.

The desk ran like clockwork. Lenders sent loan tapes — huge files containing detailed loan-level information — to Vika and her desk mates; she would load those loans into a template customized for each lender, run the numbers, organize them into a nice format for traders (a very important part, mistakes at this stage were an especially grievous offence), reconcile the numbers with ratings agencies, fix problems and respond to traders' queries. One employee would process several of those tapes a day.

The amount of attention, patience and skill required to do the job was enormous. Each tape contained tens of thousands of loans with forty to fifty columns of raw data that needed to be juggled and massaged without wasting or screwing up a single number. Final results had to be checked and rechecked numerous times. Heaven forbid the trader ends up bidding on the portfolio or gives a client info with even slightly skewed numbers — your head would roll.

This job required total immersion and focus. No lunch break, no going home before midnight, and be prepared to come in on weekends. Baruch Wolf was a boot camp, but a boot camp where serious careers were forged. Vika understood the concept, took quiet pride in the severity of the job she was doing and kept her mouth shut. A year of this, she thought, maybe a little more, and I'll move up to doing the real stuff. That was the implicit promise, an unspoken understanding among the employees. And there was never a shortage of willing freshmen lining up to replace those who moved up the food chain to sales and trading. Because of this "unspoken understanding," no one ever discussed or mentioned the "move up." Even at your annual review, you weren't supposed to let your manager know that you felt you were better than everyone by inquiring about a promotion. Vika was warned by Lenny Lucferovsky to be quiet, keep her head down and grind it out, and that's what she did. But she always wondered how those who did move up got selected, as she witnessed a few 25-year-olds who never stayed more than six months in the trenches.

Tom Bryant, Vika's new boss, got his job running the collateral desk as a result of internal reshuffling. He had a computer science background and, because analyzing large chunks of data required a programming and quantitative background, he was eventually handed this group by senior management. Part of the deal was that Tom got to keep his office on the IT floor, his original residence, and run the collateral desk from upstairs. Sitting on the trading floor would mean being bothered constantly and sucked into fights he had neither the time nor energy for, so by agreeing to take on more responsibilities, he managed to win some concessions.

Perhaps, in earlier years, he had aspired to move to the front desk like any fresh recruit entering an investment bank does, but as years passed and more aggressive guys cut in front of him or outplayed him in internal jockeying, he eventually acquiesced to his quiet, stable and well-paid niche. And why shouldn't he? He had a nice house in Long Island, a stay-at-home wife with three kids, he got to go home at 6 p.m., he was well-respected in the community and at work. Why disturb the status quo with ambition? At his age, all the major battles were behind him. He'd become accustomed to a comfortable routine, a nice title and the nice pay that comes with it, an office, responsibilities and a family. It was a perfect place to be for a man in his mid-40s.

Employees at Vika's level, although making at least twice what an average American made, were considered cannon fodder. The senior employees, who had moved up the food chain themselves, knew this and did not hesitate to pile on. Senior managers didn't have to know your name and they didn't have to care what you were working on; at any given moment, any Senior Managing Director could make his way to your desk, give you an urgent task, and you were expected to drop what you were doing and tend to this new matter. Of course, this new task, though assigned by some big guy, did not excuse you from completing the first task, which was also assigned by a no less important guy. All it meant was that you were going to have to pull another all-nighter.

Letting your direct supervisor know about this predicament was out of the question. It would be taken as a complaint, not to mention that it was a sign of "douchebaggery." Hence Tom, sitting in his office on a different floor, only had a theoretical idea about what was going on in his team. But at a place like Baruch, there was no room for micromanaging and babysitting; everyone understood that the job needed to be done with or without one's boss watching over. Vika did not dread such tasks because completing them in a fast and impeccable manner was a chance to put her name on the bigwigs' radar. But she did resent not being mentioned when she helped others with their assignments.

One such time, the head mortgage trader at Baruch Wolf, Gray Chancellor, wanted an elaborate spreadsheet put together from scratch — a task that would take a couple of days. Gray Chancellor, like all top Wall Street rainmakers, possessed a deity-like omnipresence on the trading floor even when he was absent. The sheer mention of his name among the analysts stopped all conversations mid-sentence, filled the air with awe and made everybody promptly turn back to their screens. A task from Gray Chancellor involved unlimited risks and questionable rewards. He demanded efficiency, accuracy and speed. Deliver all of it and you might be lucky enough not to hear from him; fail and you can kiss your future at the firm goodbye. The assignment was relegated to Vika by a desk mate and, naturally, she put her best efforts into it, working day and night. After checking the numbers and tables a hundred times, and adjusting the fonts and colors (the sheet was meant for an outside client, so it had to look extra pretty), Vika attached the file to an email to Gray Chancellor and put a brief message:

This is the file you requested. Please let me know if you have any questions.

Thank you.

Vika Stakhanova

She exhaled and pressed "send." Of course, she did not expect any reply. Lack of feedback meant Gray Chancellor was OK; it was only when he responded that you knew there was a problem. Still, she decided to walk over to his side of the floor to make sure everything was all right. And to sort of introduce herself.

A fixed-income trading floor is not the riveting hive of a stock exchange where everyone is screaming and gesticulating. A fixed-income trading floor is a wide-open space, sometimes as large as a football field, with rows upon rows of desks. Traders, salesmen, trading assistants, analysts and quants all sit in front of their trading stations, either parallel to one another or back-to-back. Glass offices adorn the perimeter of the floor, but they are only used for meetings, as the owners of those offices prefer to sit on the floor with their team.

Each trading station is equipped with a turret and several Bloomberg terminal screens, some on top of another. The Bloomberg terminal is a must-have tool for any trader. It's a trading and research platform that owes its name to the New York billionaire mayor. The platform costs thousands a month in subscription fees and it is a trader's primary window to the world. A trader without a Bloomberg terminal is a cook without a kitchen.

A turret — an elaborate trading communication device resembling a plane's cockpit panel with multiple buttons and switches and screens — is a switchboard to a trader's domain: All of his buddies' and clients' numbers are programmed in and assigned a button, enabling him to access anyone with walkie-talkie speed. And yet, all the cryptic operations facilitated by that extravagant technology are channeled through an old-fashioned, coil-wired, massive, black phone handset. The handset looks like a relic of the Eisenhower era, the kind of phone your grandma used to have, an odd anachronism in the sea of the state-of-the-art gadgets. The archaic sturdiness of these handsets is warranted by the traditional users' short temper. Over the history of modern-day trading floors, thousands have been slammed against tables in the manner of DeNiro assaulting a payphone in Goodfellas.

Mortgage bonds, the primary raison d'etre of all that manpower and technology, are special. These bonds are not traded through the exchanges. They are traded directly between parties, over-the-counter, or OTC. OTC products don't change hands with the speed and fluidity of the ubiquitous and highly liquid Treasury bonds. OTC products by contrast are illiquid and opaque. The price depends on someone's subjective assessment of its future behavior, and there's no unifying, standard way of valuing it.

That's the beauty of OTC products. There's a lot of money to be made on such opacity, and there's no omniscient eye in the sky, like the NYSE or the Chicago Mercantile Exchange, watching your every move. To trade an OTC bond, a trader must spend some time analyzing it, tweak a few variables and run a few scenarios. By the time he picks up the phone to trade it, his entire conversation may sound like this: "I can show you 97 and 3/4s for 25." The salesmen do most of the talking — they get their fees from selling bonds to clients. The conversations can, at times, become impassioned if there's a disagreement between parties on a bond's qualities. But analysis and intelligence gathering take up most of a trader's business hours: He has to know where similar bonds have last traded; he has to know what the risks are; and he always has to be prepared to give a customer his detailed opinion on any crap that the customer is trying to shove on him. After all, traders get paid to take positions that make or break their year-end bonus — make a mistake and you'll end up holding the colostomy bag.

Vika zigzagged through the labyrinth of rows to approach Gray Chancellor's desk. Gray Chancellor was sitting at his trading station, sphinxlike, motionless, staring at the Bloomberg screen in front of him. A man of his status required multiple screens, and he had five of them: Two with Bloomberg (one set to Bloomberg instant messages, the other on customized market data), one with Reuters, one with Excel spreadsheets and another with Outlook. His vassals sat at the adjacent desks in the same manner, quiet, eyes glued to their blinking screens, shirtsleeves rolled up, black handsets slung over their shoulders, occasionally engaging in short, coded exchanges with one another or with their turrets. There's not much talk among the traders, as most of the action happens through instant messages.

For a moment, Vika regretted walking over there, as if her sudden appearance would bring some disturbance to the Zen, this strange dance of quiet and action, calm and rush. She realized that whatever she did or said would violate this intricate dynamic. But it was too late to retreat; the traders sensed her presence and stared at her, curious at what this girl was up to. Vika approached Gray Chancellor, who was still immersed in his screens, and hesitated for a moment.

"Shoot!" someone cracked.

"Hi, I'm Vika from the collateral desk. I sent you that file you wanted. Just want to make sure everything is OK." She breathed out.

Gray Chancellor, snapped out of his meditation by this new development, lifted his head, looked at Vika, acknowledged her presence with a sullen look and, without saying a word, went back to his screens. Having received a fresh dose of reality, Vika, dumbfounded and humiliated, retreated in dead silence, but not before sneaking a what-the-fuck-are-you-looking-at glance at Gray Chancellor's posse.

***

"How am I supposed to get ahead at this place?" Vika asked Lenny.

"Vika, you fool. Just do what I told you, grind it out."

"But that's what I've been doing for two years. People

who came after me moved on to do real shit."

"Detochka, let's face it, you're not exactly from Harvard, you speak with an accent, you have a name like the girls they meet at a nightclub. You just wait your turn."

This simple truth, the stain of her questionable pedigree, had always succeeded at ending these kinds of conversations with Lenny. But it did not placate her this time.

"I work as hard as everyone else," Vika pressed on. "The data I produce is being used by everyone on the floor. I'm good at what I do. Why the fuck would anyone care about where I come from at this point?"

Lenny decided to end the conversation on a more merciful note. "Maybe they want to keep you doing what you're doing, maybe you're meant to stay there because you're so good at it."

Now she got really pissed. "So only those who suck at doing things move up? It doesn't make sense. They don't know anything about the *collateral*!" she cried and then suddenly fell quiet as it sunk in. Perhaps those taking the express lane weren't supposed to learn all the details about "the collateral."

"So this is what I'm going to do for the rest of my life?" she bitterly pondered.

***

Bonus season arrived, the day when "the Number" was announced. One by one, people were called into Tom's office. Vika was invited last and that was a bad sign, as bad news takes more time for parties to conciliate. When Tom, in a tense and almost apologetic manner — using expressions like "room for improvement," "being part of the team" and "realistic expectations" — announced her spot in the desk's pecking order, not much different from the previous year's, Vika understood where she was heading at Baruch. As he read on, she received the news with her head down, scratching off her nail polish, hyperventilating, and trying to keep a lid on her boiling resentment. Then she let her frustration be known. She lifted her red face and stared at a spot on the wall behind Tom's head.

"You're sending a very clear message," she seethed, surprising not only her manager but also herself. She couldn't contain her anger anymore. "You obviously want me to leave. You sit here in your office without ever coming down to the floor to see what's going on out there in the trenches." Since there was no turning back at this point, Vika piled on. "Realistic expectations? For all my time here, I don't remember the last time you came down on the floor to just say hello to your team, to ask how we're doing. Do you even know the amount of shit we shovel for those people down there? How can you know how late we stay every day? How do you know what I personally do to come to your conclusions about what my expectations should be?" Tears of frustration started rolling down her cheeks.

Tom, expecting an unpleasant conversation but not exactly such a drastic turn of events, mumbled, "I'm sorry, I'm very sorry."

Vika stood up, red-faced, and rushed out of the room clutching her bad-news envelope, slamming the door behind her and giving plentiful food for gossip to her onlookers. Everyone's "number" was reflected in the way they left the boss' office, prompting many lucky ones to assume a neutral or preoccupied look before emerging, so as not to spoil relations with their peers. But Vika was too upset to put on a mask, to engage in this stupid pantomime. She ran to the bathroom, where she finally broke down.

The next morning, Tom came down in a jolly mood to say good morning to everyone. To her surprise, he stopped by her desk. Vika had a news page open on her computer, which was a clear violation of an unspoken rule — no Internet on the screen when someone is behind you. Vika knew she was a goner at that point so, not giving a damn, she didn't bother to hide it.

"How's it going?" Tom said cheerfully, but with some apparent discomfort.

"Fine." Vika turned around and stared at him, waiting for the next line.

He hesitated. "Well, keep up the good work. Your folks back home must be really proud of you." By the tone of his voice, she wasn't sure whether he was being genuine or sarcastic.

"My folks are dead," Vika snipped and went back to her screen.

She waited for her bonus deposit to clear, checking her bank account all afternoon, and quit the very same day. She was, as they say on the Street, in free fall.

***

"Vika, you stupid cunt!" Lenny screamed over the phone after she informed him of this new development and sent him her resume. "You could've looked for a job while sitting on a desk. Why the fuck did you have to quit?"

"How can I describe it to you? It was physically

impossible for me to stay on that desk for even a single hour. It made me wanna puke," Vika reasoned.

"You are dumb, but I might have something for you. Later." Lenny hung up.

Chapter 4

Between the order and the confirmation
Between the bid and the ask
Falls the shadow.

— Anonymous, paying tribute to T.S Eliot

THE EARLY TO MID-AUGHTS WAS a golden age for the mortgage industry, an era of quick riches and head-spinning opportunities that kept everyone busy. No one wanted to be left out of the growing feeding frenzy. Homebuyers were snatching up houses all across the country with seemingly free money that was showered on them by unscrupulous lenders; lenders popped up like mushrooms across the country and, with unlimited credit lines to the Street's broker-dealers, unloaded those loans to Wall Street for cash, which they then used to make even more loans.

The mechanism was foolproof. Wall Street, like the crime syndicates that controlled Vegas casinos decades ago, had discovered a gold mine, a realm with no adult supervision that printed money like the Federal Reserve. There were schmucks with deep pockets on one side, lining up for the next indecipherable product the industrious PhDs would stamp out; there were suckers on the other side, leveraging themselves up to their ears, chasing the American Dream; and in the middle of it all, there were the switchboard operators, the coordinators, the puppeteers, the architects, the Houses of the Holy that kept the conveyor belt well-oiled, collecting their fees and making everyone happy. And everyone was happy: Politicians got their campaign contributions, and tax collections were up; they got to go home to their districts and brag about the economy and what they had done to make that happen. The callow got their cul-de-sac, three bedrooms, two-and-a-half baths, granite countertops, Sub-Zero refrigerators, front lawns with white picket fences and the chance to become upright citizens with no money down. The greedy got their double-digit returns. And Wall Street got its fees. What could possibly go wrong?

The Wall Street job market was reaching its apex in early 2004, especially for someone with Vika's skills. Everyone was churning out mortgage deals fueled by the abundance of cheap credit. Employers' demand for the kind of collateral knowledge Vika had acquired, toiling for almost three years at a respected shop like Baruch Wolf, trumped any potential concerns about her manner of exit from the previous job. She landed rather quickly at a proprietary desk of at Royal Oakleys PLC, a major British bank.

The proprietary desk's head, a man named Lee Henderson, cut his teeth trading agency bonds at a medium-sized bank down in Charlotte. Lee Henderson, a proud son of the American South, was an oddity among New York's polished portfolio managers. Stocky, loud and unrefined by New York standards, Lee radiated jolly debauchery, jest and irreverence toward the pompous and the serious. That included anyone with a fancy degree and letters attached to his name. Lee came from a working-class family, graduated from the University of Tennessee and got hired right out of college at First Union Bank in Charlotte, where he spent almost two decades learning the business and rising through the ranks. He lost his job during the recession of 2000-2001, but after a year of enjoying life, shooting targets and riding horses, he got a job offer from a British bank in New York, quickly accepted it and moved his family to Westchester.

Work on the buy side seemed like a walk in the park for Vika, who had received military-grade training at Baruch Wolf. The prop desk was run by three portfolio managers whose sole focus was on structured products, Vika's specialty. The desk's $1 billion portfolio consisted of mortgages, agencies and asset-backed securities. Each portfolio manager focused on a specific asset class: There was the commercial real estate guy; the asset-backed guy, who traded credit cards and auto loans; and Lee himself traded bonds issued by the quasi-governmental agencies, Fannie Mae and Freddie Mac. But those sectors, while an important part of the desk's bottom line, were subordinate to mortgage-backed securities, the primary focus of the desk and the hottest product that broker-dealers were printing, with new issues coming out every week.

During her years at Baruch Wolf, Vika, out of pure necessity, taught herself how to write code. It wasn't that hard once she figured out, by trial and error, the logic of Visual Basic. This skill saved her a lot of time. Her new desk mates, Vika discovered with glee, still copied and pasted large data sets manually and used labor-intensive maneuvers on their databases and Excel spreadsheets full of bond data. She wrote a few macros and commands that allowed her to do complex multi-step operations simply by pressing a button. Her bosses were impressed. Automating bond-analytics tools for the desk freed up time that Vika used to learn all the business aspects of bond trading. The edge that she possessed over her colleagues, with her thorough knowledge of the underlying collateral, enabled her to analyze a bond on a much deeper level. She could always present a fuller picture of the bond's future performance to Lee than other analysts on the desk who simply looked at the marketing materials provided by the broker. These were, after all, the very bonds she helped create while pooling collateral data back at Baruch Wolf.

Vika and Lee often got testy about politics, and their arguments tended to spill over into business matters. Neither of them could hold their tongues when it came to their strongest convictions. Lee, a Southern conservative and a gun owner, was certain that Vika was a Commie; Vika, in retaliation, suggested that Lee was a card-carrying member of some secret Klan chapter.

"Hey, where's Boris?" Lee would crack with a fake Russian accent.

"Where's your horse?" Vika would hit back, looking down at his signature cowboy boots. Epithets flew back and forth on the trading desk, but in some twisted way Vika welcomed the abuse — insults were a clear indication of trust. It's when you are ignored or treated politely that you should worry about your status in a group. Personal jabs between people with strong personalities have an unexpected bonding effect.

Vika, with her own deep-seated contempt for formalities and titles, while despising Lee's politics, secretly admired him. He reminded her of herself — a poor boy from the middle of nowhere with a second-tier degree, an accent and a chip on his shoulder. Vika often nagged Lee about the idea of getting her own trading limit, pointing to her analytical advantage. "What's the downside?" she figured. "He'll just say no." Eventually, her persistence paid off. One morning, she found a copy of Edwin Lefèvre's "Reminiscences of a Stock Operator" on her desk — a must-read for any aspiring trader — and, after checking with Lee that it was what she thought it was, received a modest but workable trading limit.

"Let's see your Marxist trade ideas in action," Lee said, pleased with his magnanimity. "Just don't think you're smarter than everybody else."

Vika's assessment wasn't rosy at the end of 2006. Salespeople at major broker-dealers had become more aggressive, calling every morning to chitchat about the market. In reality, they were trying to get a feel for whether Vika, Lee and the other prop desks like theirs across the Street were interested in any new "paper."[6] They weren't really interested. A jittery mood abounded among those with growing concern,

---

6 Newly issued bonds.

and there was no visible solution to the still-emerging, but evidently inescapable, wave of mortgage delinquencies. But even the pessimists didn't have any idea about the timing, the size and the ultimate impact of the upcoming apocalypse.

***

In the fall of 2006, everyone flew down to Florida for the 12th Annual Mortgage Industry Conference. Over the years, the industry's annual soiree became the hottest ticket for every player, big and small, attracting inevitable hordes of private lenders, regional banks, broker-dealers, government agencies, media, and various vendors pushing analytics software. The outing was the place to be for Who's Who of the industry. Manhattan and Greenwich, Conn., became ghost towns during these three-day bashes in the warmer climates. Trading desks were left to be tended by younger aspirants. But no major market moves were expected during those days, as all the rainmakers were busy drinking and schmoozing on yachts' decks and at nightclubs down in Miami.

The biggest parties were headlined by the Doobie Brothers and ZZ Top — darlings of the middle-aged white men. The men assumed a relaxed, giddy mood, donning print shorts and worn-out boat shoes *without* socks, the kind of fashion statement intended to evoke their boyhood of forty years ago — a time when things were simpler and carefree, when their major daily preoccupations consisted of smoking weed and playing in a garage band. In their minds, in those moments, they were still those young boys. What a great venue to show the world their playful, human side, a side carefully and deliberately buried under the suit and tie and shoptalk during the usual business conduct back in New York.

For the industry women, a younger, prettier and less numerous lot, it was a time to shine. They wore their cocktail dresses and high heels, and danced to classic rock hits as if it were disco, hoisting drinks in the air. The drunken conversations were a much-needed break — the escape from the office, the chance to get out of the suffocating suits — a pseudo liberation, an attempt at playing up their humanity and normalcy.

Vika had attended this annual gathering for several years. During her first conference, she made sure to audit all of the relevant panels, studiously scribbling bits of wisdom from industry bigwigs. But the real intel, the kind that would make one fly to Miami and endure the small talk face-to-face, always floated at private parties by the pool or at the bar, where each side tried to gauge what the other was up to. The buy side tried to figure out where to get yield, and the sell side tried to figure out what the buy side was interested in and how much money they were prepared to spend.

Nascent concerns about the "frothy" mortgage market were squashed by the optimism of big-name economists associated with big investment houses. They pulled out their graphs and charts and assured everyone that, given the historical data, there was nothing to worry about. Whatever small disruptions may occur would be over rather quickly and should be viewed as an opportunity to buy.

If the fancy charts weren't enough to convince the skeptics, the forever-elated salesmen — the professional carriers of good news — came in to finish the job: "You worry too much," they would say to the deep-pocketed fence-sitters. A good salesman knows you better than you know yourself. If you are Chinese, they will sell you yield. If you're European, they will stroke your sense of superiority. If you're an ambitious manager of an American pension fund, sitting on piles of money but bound by rules and regulations, they will find a kosher way for you to become the big swinging dick you always knew you were. And if you are an American hedge fund — a serious fund, not two guys and a Bloomberg — a smart salesman cuts the bullshit and both of you reach an understanding.

The big fish out there — pension funds, the cash-rich Chinese, the dumb Europeans, the assortment of late-to-the-party bottom-feeders with cash — are there to be used as a buffer if things go wrong for both of you. And it's not like the clients put up much resistance. Throw in a couple of steak dinners at Peter Luger, and any concern evaporates.

"Eightee percen yier! I rike!" Vika overheard a salesman describe his Chinese client's investment strategies to the delight of the group of bankers having drinks, who then burst into a smug, loud laughter. "That's all it takes, man!"

***

The conference's sunny optimism had a strange way of manifesting itself back in New York. Salesmen at Saulberg Black, the most esteemed and feared Wall Street institution, were becoming especially aggressive in late 2006 to early 2007. Lee's desk wasn't their prime client, due to its modest size and moderate appetite, thus making the Saulberg salesmen's more frequent phone calls and invitations to dinners especially suspicious. Saulberg people don't just

become friendly all of a sudden for no reason. Their Saulberg cover, Mr. Salomon, insisted on taking Lee and Vika to
a business dinner and they eventually agreed, though they
were aware that it came with some implicit expectation of
business. Both of them were curious, however, about what
those guys had to say.

The Saulberg people reserved a table at The Modern
at the Museum of Modern Art in Midtown, a popular spot
among the Wall Street deal-making crowd. First, everyone
engaged in mandatory small talk during pre-dinner drinks at
the bar, a great way to loosen up a client before shoptalk. By
the time the table was ready, Lee had reached a state of loud,
drunken joy, thundering over patrons at the bar as he spoke,
telling dirty jokes and war stories, laughing, spittle flying
from his mouth. The Saulberg traders stood around Lee, all
eyes on him, politely laughing at his jokes, like a pack of
wolves ready to close in on prey.

Vika, accustomed to friendly but dismissive treatment
from salesmen, kept quiet and observed. Saulberg guys never
got drunk, even after visibly consuming the same amount of
alcohol as their customers. Perhaps they really were a special breed. "No person can be as sharp, as self-possessed, as
polished, as worldly and knowledgeable as these guys." Vika
thought. "I mean, ask them about some abstract art or their
opinion on some vintage and not only will they oblige you
but they will also do it with such ease and eloquence and
superiority that you'll end up feeling like Charlie Brown. Or
ask them to help you put a bet on anything you want, on
any esoteric event, like a member of Kennedy family dying,
and they will deliver you a term sheet the next day. For the

right price, these guys can do anything. But if they want something from you, watch out. Your fate has been pretty much sealed." Finally, the Maître d' came and ushered the party to a table in a private room.

"So, what are you guys up to these days?" asked Mr. Salomon, assuming a swiftly sober tone, finally free to dismiss all the prerequisite niceties. A casual "What are you guys up to?" coming from a Wall Street salesman always carries a sinister ulterior motive. It means, "How much money can I make off of you?"

Lee, though in a ripe condition to do business with, was slightly disappointing: "We're selectively looking at some seasoned paper, not new issues. But to tell you the truth, we're longer than we want to be and we've been dipping our feet in this new synthetic mortgage bond index, either as a hedge or an outright short. Do you see a lot of interest in it?"

The conversation wasn't exactly heading in the direction that the Saulberg guys desired; after all, they make most of their fees from unloading newly issued bonds, or "paper," to clients, not from making markets in newly created indices.

"Making markets," one of the primary businesses of a broker-dealer, mandates a firm to fill customers' buy or sell orders any time, in any market. Market makers are like institutionalized, multibillion-dollar pawnshops: They are always in a position to buy your gold watch, and they will always show you a price for it (or a bid, as they call it), except that there's no guarantee that's the price you hoped for. But there will always be a level shown. Bo Diddley's portrayal of a pawnbroker in Trading Places is the epitome of a market maker: "In Philadelphia, it's worth fifty bucks," he says to a desperate Dan Aykroyd, who is trying to get a price on his "Rochefoucauld, the thinnest water-resistant watch in the world."

The market-making business creates a risk of accumulating undesired exposure: Imagine if 100 desperate customers show up in your store, all trying to sell you a watch. To deal with such an influx of customers, you lower the bids that you show them — that's how you protect yourself from losing money on the accumulated reserve of watches. You buy the watches, but at pennies on the dollar, hoping to sell them later at a much higher price. Such a spread is called a "bid-offer spread" and it's what keeps market makers in business. But it's a risky business because you have to buy the watch, or, "take a position." Creating and selling complex bonds, on the other hand, is a risk-free moneymaker for broker-dealers. You get paid a handsome fee and it's your customer who ends up with the exposure, not you.

A synthetic credit index — the kind that Lee was seeking to short — though an intimidating word soup to a layman, is nothing more than a collection of underlying bonds, just like Dow Jones index is a collection of underlying stocks. But unlike stocks, which are cleared through the exchanges, these indices are traded directly between the parties or, more precisely, between a Wall Street broker-dealer and a client, usually a hedge fund. It's as if our pawnbroker pooled together a collection of, say, twenty-five watches out of the hundred, and invited his customers to bet on the value of the pool going up or down, collecting a fee as customers place their bets.

It's a great model: Customers get a more liquid market and the pawnbroker, without actually producing anything of value, augments his traditional business beyond the buying and selling of *real stuff*. But the beauty of this new, out-of-thin-air (and thus "synthetic") business is that the money changing hands is real. Major Wall Street firms got into this business around 2006 by creating indices backed by mortgage bonds and corporate bonds, which allowed customers to express bullish or bearish views on the underlying bonds without having to buy or sell the actual bonds.

The liquidity of these indices provided a false sense of security. Many thought that they had found a perfect way to deal with the stand-alone, opaque, hard-to-value underlying mortgage bonds. Saulberg, as a market maker, had a duty to provide markets in this new index.

But Lee was doubly disappointing to his dinner companions. Not only was he uninterested in buying the actual bonds that Saulberg was selling, he wasn't even sure he wanted to be flat. He wanted to go short by selling the index, which meant Saulberg would have to take another side of the trade.

"Going short" occupies a special and revered place in the financial industry. Short sellers regard themselves as the cleansers of the system, an occasional forest fire that weeds out the weak and the infirm, bringing balance to the eco-system. After all, how would the market function if there were no sellers? Unlike traditional investors who buy (or "go long") assets of actual, tangible value — stocks, bonds and real estate — short sellers don't bother themselves with any such thing. To put it simply, short sellers bet against assets they *don't even own*. How does one sell something he doesn't own? That's where those synthetic indices come in. You pick up the phone, call any reputable broker, ask him for a bid on a particular index, hit it and you're done. Your position is now "negative," or, in a trader's lingo, "short" — it gains in value when the underlying collection of bonds loses value.

Short selling is akin to buying an insurance policy. Indeed, short sellers themselves like to refer to such bets as "buying insurance" or "buying protection." They pay a fee upfront, and later, when everything goes to shit, they come and collect. And there are no bounds on what they can short; their position is not limited to the value of the asset they bet against. When a homeowner buys an insurance policy on his house, he has a "flat," or "neutral," position according to a short seller's worldview. If his house burns down, the homeowner gets back only the value of the house and not a penny more. Win some, lose some, flat in the end. When a short seller buys insurance on a hypothetical house, he plans to make money when the house burns down because he doesn't own that house. He gets paid without losing any asset value in the process, unlike the homeowner. And if there are hundreds of short sellers all betting against the same house, as they rarely travel alone, then that house is doomed — too much money to be made. Who cares about the poor guy living in it?

And who was selling such insurance? Insurance companies and a few investment banks that should have known better.

By the fall of 2006, the die had been cast for many

preeminent and respectable institutions. For a few dollars upfront, they wrote billions in insurance contracts to a bunch of prescient and shrewd short sellers who came in the form of hedge funds. There was no easy way to get out of such a massive, bad trade. Insurance sellers resembled pawnbrokers who failed to manage their risk correctly, selling insurance on too many watches that turned out to be fake Rolexes.

In about a year, everyone would realize that those synthetic indices were backed by fake Rolexes. And when the short sellers came to collect, those centuries-old embodiments of prudence, those once proud, stalwart institutions, would become roadkill. They would become fodder for the befuddled and clueless anchors on the 11 o'clock evening news and on the morning talk shows. And Saulberg Black, more than anything, didn't want to be that roadkill.

Neither did Lee. Now, at the dinner, Lee wanted to go short and the Saulberg guys were not pleased.

But Saulberg traders, a resourceful bunch who don't get paid multimillion-dollar bonuses for nothing, wouldn't be Saulberg traders if they didn't have some tricks up their sleeves, even against such an unfortunate turn of events. If Lee wants to trade that index, they will facilitate it for him. Here and now. Anything for a client.

"I can show you a locked market," said a young trader, smiling, but with cold, probing eyes.

A boring client dinner just got interesting. According to an unspoken traders' tradition, a client can't back away from a locked market. When a trader shows a locked market to a client, he only shows one level, one price, without knowing what the client is going to do. But with this move, although exposing himself to the risk of ending up with the undesired position, the market maker shifts the burden of decision-making onto the client. Now the client must sell (hit it) or buy (lift it) at that level. For a client, to refuse the trade is to acquire the status of a douchebag, to become the butt of jokes among the Street guys. For some, it's worse than losing money. Now they had Lee right where they wanted him: Drunk, ready to make a trade, with no place to retreat, bound by gentlemanly rules, a perfectly executed bait-and-switch, custom-tailored for Lee's persona by these young, sly Saulberg guys.

"OK." Lee was ready to gamble. "What do you have for 06-1 BBB?"

"What size?" the trader asked.

"Twenty-five," Lee said, but it was way past time to be cautious.

"Oh, come on, Lee. Twenty-five? For a man of your stature? Let's do fifty!"

"Eh, fuck it, let's do fifty," Lee roared, himself beginning to enjoy this one-upmanship.

"I'll show you 06-1 BBB at ninety-five," the young trader said.

Vika, having all the index levels in her head, knew that that piece, the BBB-rated tranche, traded at a 95-96 bid-offer that day. The locked market of 95, where Lee could buy or sell, was way too low, indicating Saulberg's trade preferences, or "axe." This Saulberg trader obviously wanted Lee to buy at 95 by showing him the kind of level Lee wouldn't be able to get anywhere else. "The big question is, do we really want to own $50 million BBB-rated tranche of a mortgage index at a time when we were looking to short it? Hit it, you shit-kicking redneck!" Vika thought.

"Hit it!" she yelled.

"I'll lift you at ninety-five for fifty," Lee said, and everyone except Vika burst into congratulatory yells and high fives. Now dinner could proceed as usual. Lee came to a pawnbroker to place a bet against a pool of watches, but the pawnbroker, knowing something bad about the product, showed such a low price that the poor customer ended up buying a watch instead. The Saulberg guys got what they wanted.

***

As the market moved slightly down the next morning, Lee, hungover but disciplined, took that position off at a small loss. Vika was eager to wisecrack but, in a rare display of situational prudence, decided that perhaps it was better not to make any sarcastic comments.

Curious, however, about Saulberg's axe, she decided to get some market color from her buddy Neal Bitterman. A nice Jewish guy from Queens in his late 30s, Neal was Vika's cover at a big European broker-dealer. They went for drinks a few times, once ending up at an ambiguous, drunken, late-night goodbye on the cobblestone streets of the Meatpacking District. But Neal didn't press for more than a kiss on the cheek, and explained to an incredulous Vika that she wasn't Jewish enough for him.

"Oh, come on, dude. We won't tell your mother," she would retort impatiently. But Neal was adamant. She got mad and told him, "Go fuck yourself and don't call me anymore." But Neal, finding her candid manner refreshing, always called her up for a friendly chat. In the end, while still puzzled by his strange shtick, Vika accepted his friendship. "He's just a weirdo," she concluded.

"Dude," Neal said over the phone, "if you wanna get the full picture, we can meet at Campbell's after work and discuss. It's kind of a long story."

After work, they met at Campbell Apartment, a cocktail lounge near Grand Central Terminal.

"So, what's the long story?" Vika wasn't going to waste any time with small talk.

"Basically, there's a big correlation trade going on. Saulberg is simply in the middle of it. There are hedge funds looking to short the mortgage market and, in order to do that in size, they need to create as many deals as possible and find somebody to take the other side of the trade."

"What is a correlation trade?"

"Well, it's when you buy one tranche of a deal and sell the other tranche of the same deal. The point is to try to make more money on one side of the trade than you lose on the other or, if things don't go according to plan, to at least break even. So, hedge funds go long the equity[7] piece and short the mezzanine[8] piece of a deal. It's rather foolproof. The only way they will lose money is if the equity piece is wiped out and the mezzanine piece stays intact. And the chances of that happening are nil. Essentially, they have no downside. So, as soon as the mezz piece starts taking on water, they start cashing in."

---

7   The lowest, most risky slice of a mortgage bond. It's also known as "first-loss piece."

8   The middle tranche of a mortgage bond. It takes on losses only after the equity tranche has been wiped out.

"Why can't they just short the mezzanine tranche outright?"

"You see, the equity piece pays, like, a 20 percent yield before it goes bust. And they know it will go bust, they just want to collect a few fat payments from it before it dies a horrible death. Then they use the cash from that shit piece to buy protection on a mezzanine tranche, like BBB, which they also hope will deteriorate eventually. Considering the crap that went into those deals, it's not a far-fetched scenario. So, this is the perfect kind of trade for somebody who thinks things are so bad that the losses will reach into mezzanine and perhaps even senior tranches, but can't figure out the exact timing of the Armageddon."

"So they don't care if they lose money on the equity piece?"

"Nope. The equity piece is so thin that the hedgies won't feel any pain when it pops, and they're OK with losing $1 million in principal there if down the road it means making hundreds of millions. What they are really after is the mezzanine. The more the deal deteriorates, the more money they will make. Also, somebody has to buy that equity piece in order for a deal to close. Hedge funds want the deal to close so they can short it. So, for them, buying that equity piece and taking a hit on it is, like, a small price to pay to be able to be massively, spectacularly short elsewhere."

"So it's sort of like spending $200K to build a shaky house and then buying a bunch of insurance contracts on it that will yield $20 million when it collapses?"

"Yeah, I guess you can use that analogy. And to add insult to injury, they are collecting rent in the meantime."

"What shrewd motherfuckers!" Vika marveled at the beauty of the trade. "And how big is this trade, you think?"

"It's all leveraged. Tens, but more likely hundreds of billions. Many hedgies out there are doing it."

"And who's on the other side? Wait, don't tell me. Insurance companies and pension funds?"

"Correctamundo. And the reason pension funds can be sucked into that trade is that they see hedge funds buying this crap and are tricked into thinking everything is tip-top."

"Dear God! Have mercy on us. You realize the implications of it?"

"Yeah, no shit."

"Dude, don't send any more bonds my way. Fuck that shit. I'll be hitting your bids from now on."

"Ha. I never considered your desk a serious buyer anyway. CDO managers are sucking everything dry before you even wake up in the morning. But you're welcome to use our index markets, sure. I get paid either way."

After drinks, Neal and Vika strolled to Vanderbilt Avenue and 42nd Street. Vika hailed a cab.

"Aren't you coming downtown with me?" She decided to give it another try.

"No, dude, I have to be at my desk at 7 tomorrow. Gotta get some sleep."

"You'll sleep at my place."

"Vika, you're a crazy shiksa. And I'm looking for a nice Jewish girl."

"What are you, religious or something?"

"I'm just mindful of my heritage."

"We'll use protection. We won't contaminate your heritage."

"I'm just not that kind of guy."

"You mean you're gay?"

"I'm not gay. Let's just say I'm more traditional than you."

"Guys like this don't exist. Not in New York. There's something wrong with you."

"I know it's hard for you to wrap your head around, but perhaps I really am just a nice guy. Why don't you entertain the possibility?"

Vika sighed. "OK, nice guy, have a good night then. With your hand."

She got into a taxi.

"Broadway and 8th," she barked at a taxi driver. "And take the 5th down, not Broadway."

***

The first ominous signs came in January when the market became erratic, moving 2 to 3 percentage points down and up, where previously it had moved only a fraction of a point. Vika, having observed the performance of hundreds of bonds, was way too familiar with the kind of underlying collateral that went into those bonds and saw no possible remedy to the worsening housing defaults. She thought the dislocation would not be cured overnight or even in months. So, whatever position she entered was a short, a bet on a move down.

It was scary at first. But the fear only prompted Vika to plow through, to immerse herself in this combat of nerves.

She welcomed the adversity. It allowed her to exploit all of her previously untapped resources. To her surprise, she found the market disorder intellectually stimulating. It made her feel alive. Routine is debilitating for an impatient, active mind, but turmoil is a gift that reawakens some dormant forces.

As she started to book profits, a new, exhilarating feeling began to displace her familiar emotions. A thirst for the hunt, for victory, now preoccupied her. Constant ruminations on the dynamics of the markets, the players, the government, now consumed her every minute. And anyone who had nothing to say about the markets quickly lost her interest. "They have no clue what's going on and I'm just too busy to explain it to them," she thought. "They lie on a sunny beach, oblivious to the fact that the water has already receded and the tsunami is forming on the horizon."

Vika met every new headline about another small lender biting the dust with private celebration, even glee. Any bad news was good news for her. Now that she got a taste of the hunt — the long-sought outlet, the medium to channel all her skills — it breathed new meaning into her everyday motions. The results were immediate, the gratification swift. The outside world had ceased to exist.

The biggest secret that traders don't want the world to know is that anyone with a more or less sane disposition can do what they're doing. The trick is getting access to the trough, to the P&L, to the "book." The road toward it is tough, treacherous and crowded. On the way there, you will be misled into believing that in order to be a trader you must have a physics PhD, or know how to write code and build models, or have a top-school MBA, or, when all else fails, just be a young Caucasian male. But in the end, it doesn't matter *who* made it to the top. In the end, it all comes down to merely placing a bet. The ideas of those who made it become validated by the platform on which they stand, by the levers they can pull.

Becoming a trader is like reaching a craps table on your twenty-first birthday with your rich uncle's money in your hand; without that craps table and without that money, you are a nobody. Without a seat and a desk and a Bloomberg terminal, your ideas aren't worth shit. Whatever you do at home with your 401(k) doesn't matter; your trades have to be big and visible to everyone or, at the very least, to those who dispense your reward at the end of the year. If you know how to drive but don't have a fancy car to demonstrate your prowess, no one cares about your prowess. The platform becomes a powerful communication tool: One should have great ideas and only act on them using a big podium.

The "book" is the medium through which you can communicate your entire worldview and let fools know that they're fools without needing to actually say anything. If you're right on your trades, you will become rich; you can then fancy yourself to be Bruce Wayne or John Pierpont Morgan or James Bond. You can establish scholarships in your name and start foundations to spread your gospel — conservative, liberal, libertarian, whatever floats your boat. If you're wrong, well, you won't get more money from your uncle, but you will gain an invaluable experience. You will earn your bona fides to speak about the irrational players and stupid monetary policies and dysfunctional government, and still insist that your general strategy was correct and would most likely work next year. And you'll probably be right, too, at some point. You can't lose! Becoming a trader is the greatest trade of all.

In this newfound realm, Vika had developed a new moral compass. Indecisiveness was an especially grievous offense according to her new standards. One should do the analysis, pick a side and stick with it — not question it afterward, not wring hands and second-guess. But those who overanalyzed and became paralyzed by the weight of their knowledge as a result immediately made it into Vika's mental black book. Those chin-stroking pointy-heads who can argue both sides just don't have the stones to take the plunge. They mask their fear and inaction with perpetual pettifoggery.

"If my grandma had balls, she would have been my grandpa," Vika liked to say, mocking the absurd mental con-tortions of someone complaining about the way a trade had gone. "Take a loss and move on. What use is it to dwell?" Stepping into the abyss requires a certain skill, a special mental disposition, an ability to let go. This philosophy of letting go, of abandon, fascinated Vika. Once she'd decided on a trade, she would fight off the doubts. And with shaky, sweaty hands, Vika would pick up the phone and make a trade. And then… the weightlessness, the fall.

Why is it that we claim to want certainty? Only fools and cowards seek certainty. Certainty is a dead end; it's a rich old widow living out the rest of her days on the Upper East Side with a little dog and big memories. Unless you are a senior citizen, you'll go nuts after a few weeks of knowing what the rest of your life will bring. You'll die of boredom. But uncertainty is what keeps us alive. It is that flip of a coin, that brief moment when it's in the air or spinning on its side, that snaps us out of our daily stasis. Some invisible Odds Gods are giving you a chance to become better, smarter, richer. What fun it is to get paid if you earned it by the skin of your teeth, by the close call. And how dreadful it is to shoot fish in a barrel. Exposure to uncertainty earns you membership in a select tribe: You are a Padawan mastering the Force. Once the trade is on, once the die has been cast, you're in a parallel, auspicious universe. There's only one way forward and there are only two ways out: Take it off at a loss or take it off at a profit.

There's no color in the events — no meaning, good or bad. Booms and crashes do not carry biases. Events just happen without any one of us in mind, without any lessons attached. Politicians, moralists and common folk live to find meaning in the events. But a good trader doesn't assign moral meaning to either move. He doesn't seek the destruction of his enemies nor affirmation of his macroeconomic worldview. A good trader doesn't seek to prove everyone wrong, he seeks to make money. People losing their jobs and homes are just events, market dislocations that, while unfortunate, have to be viewed as just another trade. And while fools are preoccupied with looking for a scapegoat, sages are busy figuring out the next step, the source of the next big move.

But, when all is said and done, what matters is the position, the skin in the game. Not having a position was anathema to Vika, it was time wasted. What good is it to have an opinion on the market without putting any money to work?

True to her principles, she made sure to have a position on a daily basis. Vika's returns topped 35 percent at the close of 2007. Not entirely John Paulson's territory, but for a first serious year of trading, it was something to take pride in. She expected a good bonus, but Lee exceeded even her boldest estimates. When, on bonus day, Vika restively plunged into a chair in Lee's office and gave him a testy look instead of a "hello," he slid a piece of paper across the desk with a number a few dollars short of seven figures.

"Put some of it away for a rainy day," he said, enjoying the number's effect on a clearly stunned Vika.

"What, you think I'm some kind of degenerate gambler?" Vika scoffed, finally collecting herself.

"I'm just saying, this trade of yours is too crowded now, not to mention that it's run its course. It might get a little rocky going forward, that's all I'm saying. We had a good year, the kind of year people wait their whole lives for. Very possibly, it was the best year of our entire careers. After a year like this, it's all downhill. Trust me, I've been in this business long enough to know."

"Sure, boss." Vika stood up to leave, but then let her stern demeanor lapse for a moment. "Hey, Lee. Uh, thank you."

"No, thank you. Good job!"

***

Paradoxically, a good bonus — a price tag indicating one's value, meant to retain a good worker — also becomes a powerful incentive for an opportunistic and disloyal Wall Street soul to seek even greener pastures with even bigger responsibilities and bigger P&L. Headhunter Lenny was one of the first people Vika called and, after a long pause, he told her that she'd "arrived." Vika met Lenny for drinks in mid-March 2008 to discuss the possibilities. The timing, however, was most unfortunate. Their meeting took place as Baruch Wolf, her former employer, was teetering on the verge of collapse, and market disruptions consumed their conversation.

"Their stock is at the bottom, it can't possibly go any lower," said Lenny, who was thinking of buying some of Baruch's stock on the dip.

Vika, by staring at Bloomberg all day, by hearing the Street chatter and sensing the general gloomy, almost panicky, stomach-churning feel in the markets, wasn't so sure it was a good idea.

"I don't know, Lenny, you should see their CDS spreads.[9] They are triple the level of any of the other guys. And today we were told from above not to enter any trades with them. We are to cease all trading with Baruch. No one wants to have them as counterparty anymore. What we're seeing is unprecedented. It can't be cured by any reassuring talk from management or even by raising capital. It's a matter of trust and they have no trust left, no one will lend them anything."

"Whatever, it's at historic lows. It's just a cheap option," Lenny countered, dismissing or not willing to acknowledge the seriousness of the situation described by Vika.

"You know, I'm glad to see them collapse," she suddenly said, then paused to get her thoughts together. "They're getting what they deserve. They used to praise themselves on

---

9   A measure of a company's creditworthiness. The higher (or wider) the spread, the worse shape the company is in.

being this meritocracy, taking in all the scrappy kids no one else wanted — you know, hungry, driven kids who are not afraid to do the dirty work, yearning to become rich. And what did they turn out to be? A bunch of arrogant crooks. I played by the book. I worked hard, stayed late, always delivered on time and kept my mouth shut, just like you told me to, but in the end I wasn't good enough for them." She took a sip and then grinned bitterly. "I guess I had the wrong last name for that shop."

Lenny chuckled. "Yeah, perhaps you did."

She continued, getting more agitated. "But I was that person. I was that scrappy kid. And they looked at me and didn't see it. I was that kid!" People at the bar began to stare at her.

"Well, perhaps you didn't make a hard enough effort to show it to them," Lenny said, shrugging his shoulders.

"Fuck 'em!" Vika concluded and finished her drink.

Chapter 5

They won't let me... I can't be... good!
– Fyodor Dostoyevsky, Notes from the Underground

ALL SELF-DOUBT EVAPORATES AFTER A good bonus. A good bonus is the answer to all existential questions. It's the reason for and the purpose of life, a tangible expression of one's power. How does one deal with sudden power, power not of words but of action? From Vika's new perspective, it all depended on what kind of action. The actions of anyone outside her industry became trite and boring. Even doctors and lawyers had second-tier professions according to her new worldview because, though well paid and in demand, they lacked something transcendent, some magic lever with which to move boundaries.

"What do they know, what does anyone know?" Vika

thought, gasping, squeezing her stress toy, watching the market come unglued yet another 4 or 5 percentage points a day. "The world as we know it is ending, but they still go about their business, making plans, having babies."

Life outside work, the time when others released the tension and tended to the wounded nerves that accumulated during the workweek, provided no relief for Vika. Aggressive and focused at work but unable to switch off her professional persona, she became insufferable during off-hours. She engaged in the usual weekend rites like shopping and brunch with girlfriends, but in an almost mechanical manner, without taking any pleasure in it; if snapped out of her aloof state by a chatty waiter or a shop girl, she became annoyed and snooty.

Shopping, a sacred ritual of any woman during hours of leisure, while being studiously observed by Vika on a regular basis, stopped being gratifying. No, she surely could appreciate the experience of getting herself another bag or a pair of shoes, but it did not bring the same bang as before. At Barneys — Vika's preferred shopping venue, as she insisted on maintaining a slightly rebellious and cutting-edge fashion streak even with her office attire — she would give a menacing stare to the hovering salesperson to make him disappear. They usually got the message. But the utility of fancy things, she found with dismay, was becoming more and more marginal.

"What's the point in looking good and polished? To impress friends?" The answer eluded her, so, to bury those lingering thoughts, she pressed on with the usual routine: Work, gym, occasional travel and a cursory interest in art

— which, on further examination, wasn't an interest at all but a chance to attend gallery openings, get drunk and amuse herself with the banality of other people's daily concerns.

Vika looked for thrills by traveling to exotic destinations during her mandatory two-week vacations.[10] While traveling through Cambodia and Vietnam, Vika, wearing white silk pants and Tod's moccasins she purchased for $400 during the layover in Hong Kong, fancied herself to be a sort of female Captain Willard. Locals didn't cooperate. On a boat tour of the Mekong Delta, she tried to entertain her local guide and a couple of hippie German tourists by quoting Apocalypse Now, only to be met with blank stares.

"Charlie don't surf," she said in frustration, as no one around seemed to appreciate her wit.

"Who is Charlie?" her confused guide inquired.

On a tour through Scottish castles, Vika's plans to enjoy the pastoral scenery and contemplate on medieval culture and epic battles by listening to the Lord of The Rings soundtrack were ruined by her accompanying girlfriends, who insisted on playing Russian pop songs nonstop in the car. She attempted to deal with this grating dichotomy by enlightening them on the narrative and significance of the book, its powerful allegories, and how it's not about elves and orcs at all. Despite her best rhetorical efforts, her words didn't have the desired effect.

"They just walk and fight, walk and fight. Where's the sex? And maybe shit wouldn't get out of hand if they all just stayed home," was the overwhelming verdict.

---

10   A trader must take an uninterrupted two-week vacation once a year for compliance purposes.

She eventually managed to talk her girlfriends into letting her play the "Battle of Evermore."[11]

"A good gateway drug," she thought of her choice. Given the chance and hoping for greater effect, Vika sang along — about the Queen of Light and the Dark Lord — missing the notes, but compensating for it in passion. Still, she failed to generate any interest, just a lot of giggles.

"Let's find Vika some nice Scottish goblin for tonight," someone suggested. "Let them play Mordor!" Everyone burst into cackle.

"Fuck you guys!" Vika gave up. "I should have just brought my headphones," she brooded.

Her girlfriends both fascinated and bored her with their talk of endless and resolution-free relationships.

"Why can't they just either move in with the guy or abandon him altogether? Why be tortured by a self-imposed, self-conceived, perpetual tug-of-war?" Vika wondered. "Perhaps they just don't want to make a decision. Perhaps this paralysis is what they seek after all. It spares them regret later and leaves them the option to blame others. Or maybe they just love the drama — it keeps brunch conversations lively. Amazing how people worship the freedom to make choices but are paralyzed when it comes to actually making them. They dream of amassing all the chips at the table but are incapable of moving all-in."

Dating was a problem for Vika too, but not because she couldn't make up her mind. She quickly lost interest if her

11   A Led Zeppelin song that makes references to J.R.R. Tolkien's *The Lord of the Rings*.

date couldn't render a coherent opinion, by her standards, on markets or politics; she couldn't possibly go to bed with an idiot. One date, with a hedge fund manager who had suspiciously never married by his late 40s, was a success. By the end of the dinner, they were discussing Grover Norquist and U.S. tax policies. They mostly disagreed, but it didn't matter. "He's sufficiently corrupt to have a good time with," Vika thought. In the back of a taxicab after dinner, however, he buckled up, prompting Vika — drunk, festive and in high dudgeon — to make cruel fun of him all the way to his apartment.

"You probably have some lame basis trade[12] on too." She laughed, further deriding his needless caution.

The hedgie lived on the twenty-fifth floor of the Trump World Tower in the East 40s with a panoramic view of the East River. A giant neon Pepsi-Cola sign from across the river in Long Island City lit up the dim bedroom.

"Nice view," Vika said. "But shitty location," she added. The hedgie chuckled.

"For someone pushing 50, he's not that bad," Vika thought when they got into bed. "But there must be a reason why he's single." She looked at the picture on his nightstand where he and an older lady were smiling into the camera.

"Who's that?" Vika asked.

"That's me and my mother."

"Oh, I see. There's a mother there," Vika thought as she turned away and looked out the window, trying not to laugh. He pulled a plastic bag filled with neatly rolled doobies from

---

12   A low-risk, low-return trade. It usually involves being long an asset and simultaneously long protection on it.

his nightstand drawer and lit one up.

"So, what's your vice?" he asked.

"Definitely not pot," Vika replied.

"What is it then?"

"I'm still trying to figure it out."

"Why don't we figure it out together?"

Vika gave him an "are you serious?" look. "I don't think you're the type to do it with."

"Don't be such a meanie."

Vika took the roach from his hand, inhaled, thought for a while, then spoke.

"I remember how, many years ago, when I was still at Baruch Wolf, I went to one of those 'Women on Wall Street' events. Hillary, freshly elected as a New York senator, was headlining the event. I was overwhelmed by all the feel-good sermons coming from the panelists and excited to be a part of this empowered sisterhood. I thought everything was possible, just like they said. Hell, I was still in my 20s, ha! I walked over to Hillary's table to get an autograph. She was surrounded by a crowd of journalists and well-wishers. I asked one of the journalists for a pen, which she reluctantly parted with, and elbowed my way to Hillary. She signed my piece of paper while talking to someone else. I found her cold and distant. Cold and distant, you know? Hillary! A shining beacon of hope for all of us striving career girls. I felt let down. It was only much later that I realized what that was all about. She's not supposed to be warm and bubbly and approachable; she's not a server at Denny's, you know? All these bullshit theatrics… It was a big revelation to me. That encounter taught me more than all those stupid women's conferences taken together. Maybe our mistake is that we try too hard to be 'good.' What use is it to be good? Especially now."

"So, your vice is being a bitch?"

"No. My vice is winning. At all costs. If that makes me a bitch in the process, so be it."

"That's an interesting vice. And an interesting choice of role models."

"She's not exactly a role model. I just like her attitude. She doesn't give a fuck what we think of her. I like that."

"What about you?"

"What about me?" Vika took another drag.

"You obviously have everything figured out."

"No need to be facetious, but I do. You can hedge your ass all you want, but I'm riding this market all the way to the bottom."

"Risky. Bid-offer will kill you."

"If you're afraid of wolves, you shouldn't go into the woods."

"What?"

"It's a Russian proverb."

"What does it mean?"

"It means if you're afraid of life, you should probably stay at home and do nothing. But you hedge fund guys, you really are something. You think of yourselves as these fearless mavericks, but you only put on trades that have guaranteed returns and zero risk. You raid others for value without risking anything. You devise all these elaborate schemes where you get all the upside and everyone else gets the downside.

First you shoot all the wolves and only then go into the forest, spreading myths all around about your 'bravery.'"

"You're just jealous that it's not you. You would do the same thing if you had the chance."

"Me?! I prefer an honest fight."

"Honest fight? You think that you trading your index is somehow beneficial to humanity?"

"Unlike you, I take real risk. I risk real money!"

"But if you could make money without that risk, you would do that."

"How do you know if you're good at what you do if you are not risking anything? How will you know if you're deserving of the outcome?"

"Who cares? This is the Holy Grail of trades — zero downside and unlimited upside. You'd do it in a second if such an opportunity landed on your lap. Are you honestly saying you would just let it pass? Spare me the sanctimony. We have already established that winning at all costs is what you do. You want to think you're different, but you're not."

Vika paused, at a loss for words. "I gotta go," she said quickly.

"Already? I was just beginning to be entertained."

"What am I, a clown?"

"Ha! I find your insults… endearing."

"OK. Bye."

"Call me."

"Sure."

Vika never called the hedgie back. But she couldn't quite discard his flippant comment about her motivations.

"What can possibly be done under such an unraveling scenario?" Vika would ponder. "At this point, all I can do is take advantage of the situation. I have a perspective and access to tools to act on that perspective. I did not create this mess and the least I can do is take care of myself. And later, I will be able to help others, to donate to charity, to become a *better person*. But now I have to take advantage of the situation that the fools created. I can't sit idle, there's too much money to be made."

***

Market dislocations intensified in an unprecedented manner in the summer of 2008. It became clear to Vika that this meltdown would not be confined merely to the mortgage market. Now it wasn't simply a question of mortgage delinquencies and of bonds losing value. Too many factors would have a snowball effect: The high leverage of all major players, unfunded credit-default swaps, and credit events[13] creating domino effects — no one would be spared, not even solid, prudent, conservative institutions. Everyone would have to raise cash, and the only way to do that is to get rid of assets, even good ones.

The magnitude of the upcoming apocalypse made sober minds grim. Daily adrenaline rushes kept Vika awake at night, the dreadful time with no distractions, no newsfeed to keep her away from morbid thoughts. Having a position meant being in a state of constant anxiety. Volatility was reaching levels never before seen, with bid-offer spreads, even on a supposedly liquid index, approaching 3 to 5 points. Vika couldn't hold her positions for too long and

---

13   A failure of a company to pay interest or principal on its obligations.

continue making money on them. Even if she was right on the direction of the trade, she still had to clear a few points just to break even. But she couldn't stop and didn't want to stop. Idleness meant no bonus; it also meant boredom.

"And what else could I possibly be doing? No other industry can award me the same opportunities, the same lifestyle. You're either on Wall Street or you're a bum, and there's nothing in between. I'm in this cult from which no one wants to be rescued. All I can do is double my efforts and plow forward. And the fools... well, the fools are there for us to fleece and then to show mercy." These rationales provided just enough mental numbness to get her through yet another day.

***

"And what do they know? They don't know how close they are to the abyss," Vika thought on an occasional subway ride home, looking at the passengers who, oblivious to the extent of their frailty, bantered and laughed and read stupid books or were on their way to some stupid park to sit on the grass or whatever.

They didn't know what she knew; they couldn't even begin to fathom the workings of the System that affected their every move. "How can they be so carefree?" Vika pondered with disgust at their state of ignorant bliss, their lack of consciousness. "They wake up in the morning, take a long subway ride to work, do their monotonous, meaningless tasks, take an hour lunch, leave work at 5, take a long subway ride home and finish their day watching sitcoms, cooking dinner and dreaming of a retirement right out of a Cialis commercial. Day in and day out. Year in and year out. And then what? What's the point? Are we meant to be born, pay our bills and then die?" Vika's gaze froze on the advertisement above the seats.

Imagine 30 years or more of doing what you love.
Time to think of retirement.
Prudential.

"Thirty years?! What could I possibly do for thirty years? Run on the beach in slow motion in a flowing tunic? Buy a fucking easel and paint?"

An old man entered the subway car, interrupting her ruminations. This was a truly ancient man, well into his ninth decade; his bended-knee gait propped up by oversized sneakers, high-waist pants saggy around his flat rear, weathered brown suit jacket with side pockets bulging from years of use, a square trucker hat with the "Korean War Veteran" logo. Holding on to the rail with shaky arthritic hands, he made his way into the seat in front of Vika and, with sad, watery eyes behind thick, oversized glasses, stared at an empty space before him, contemplating.

Watching old farts, or "old men porn" as Vika called it, was her secret hobby, a small obsession even, that always made her spellbound. There was something captivating and endearing about old age. Unlike beautiful girls or young jocks, old men do not expect attention and, oblivious to the world around them, give ample opportunity for a curious observer to ogle. For Vika, the arresting melancholy of watching a lonely grandpa was more penetrating than watching a lonely grandma. She wasn't quite sure why. Perhaps because old men never form a peer support group the way old ladies do. Old men were never meant to make it that far. Alone and lost like a small child separated from his parents at a train station, they wander around not knowing where to go, what to do.

"Here is a man who doesn't know and doesn't care about what's going on, about the world coming to an end. But even if he knew, with all the intricate details that I know, he still wouldn't care," Vika thought. "How nice would it be not to care."

Suddenly despondent, Vika felt an unwelcome knot in her throat but was unable to take her eyes off him. The old man's unconscious but piercing communiqué of infinite sorrow and quiet resignation spoke of a forlorn world that Vika didn't dare to imagine. The cool air of the subway car became suffocating. Embarrassed at her own sudden weakness and grateful for her train stop to approach, she jumped out of the cool train, inhaled the thick stench of sticky New York subway heat and, for reasons she couldn't quite explain, began to weep uncontrollably. "Fuck!" she said out loud, angry with herself for being such a wimp.

On the way home, she stopped at a local deli. The two Mexican immigrants tending the counter knew Vika but had learned to tread ground carefully with her — she usually had only two modes of doing business, morose or snippy.

"Two poppy seed bagels," Vika said, looking at her Blackberry and still thinking of that old man, but no one heard her. One guy behind the counter was filling other orders, the other, sitting down for a small break, was unable to see her. Vika, impatient, looked around and, spotting the guy sitting on a chair, repeated louder: "Can I have two poppy seed bagels?"

"Sorry, miss." The guy sprang from the chair. "What do you say, two bagels?"

"Yes." Vika gave him a cold stare. "Two. Poppy. Seed. Bagels. No toasted. No nothing."

"Here we go." The guy swiftly put the two bagels into a brown paper bag, looked at her and smiled. "Good night, miss."

Vika rolled her eyes, grabbed the bag and, without saying a word, walked out.

"I'm a despicable person," she thought in anguish.

***

In the fall, the bottom fell out. It's not like it came completely unexpected. Things were going south for a few months now. But, like a crew on a sinking ship sensing the inevitable but refusing to believe it, everyone continued to pump water — the only thing they knew how to do — hoping to somehow make it ashore. "What doesn't kill us makes us stronger" was their mantra in the face of grim news.

But when Lehman and AIG went down, and the possibility of losing 85 cents on the dollar on their derivatives contracts stared everybody in the face, the customary snark and defiance with which Wall Street warriors routinely greet adversity dissipated. Aspirants for elder statesmanship got really scared. This time the shit was about to get real. The Wall Street and D.C. crowds, bred on military and biography books, knew that today was that day — the day to pick the right side of history.

Alas, no one had the bullet points and the procedure manual at hand. Those few with the knowledge of the underlying dynamics froze in terror. The situation was now beyond their control and there was no time to be creative or to sit and wait. Somebody had to take the reins and explain the repercussions of inaction to those country bumpkins in Congress who held the purse strings. So, a handful of bigwigs went to D.C., opened their books to incredulous G-men at the Treasury and the Fed, and asked for a rescue.

The politicians, not sure about what they saw when they peeked under Wall Street's skirt but certain it was something profound, hesitated for a moment, but when the realization sunk in that if they didn't act, by Monday there wouldn't be an economy to run, they pulled the trigger. These guys at the Treasury and the Fed weren't fucking around. The heavyweights' entrance into the history books was assured with the $700 billion price tag.

Chapter 6

GLOOM DESCENDED OVER THE FONTAINEBLEAU Miami Beach one balmy weekend in October 2010. Thousands of the surviving mortgage industry insiders flocked to the posh oceanfront resort to attend the annual Mortgage Industry Conference. Everyone treaded carefully, afraid to say anything spontaneous, aware of their own fragility but remaining devout about it, attached to it — as if this brittle, shaky but familiar ground was preferable to the encroaching unknown. Gallows humor enlivened the scaled-down parties, but laughs were tense and conversations jumpy. Industry boom, a somewhat recent history, now seemed light-years away. The only mental trick that participants used to mitigate the overwhelming fear was abundant self-mockery, dark humor that implied they were shaped by forces beyond their control. Although, when it came to discussing business, all hints of jest evaporated. Conversations took a subdued, dour tone and moved to the dark secluded corners or outside.

Government actions dominated the discussion among attendees. Vika supported the bailout, although she preferred not to be vocal about it. She'd seen a run on the banks before, in Moscow in the early 1990s. Back then, her entire savings, several hundred rubles inherited from her mother, were wiped out. For years after that, she lamented not having spent it on a new TV set. The possibility of such a scenario happening twice in her lifetime was unfathomable. So she preferred the idea of sober statesmen in suits making decisions in proverbial smoke-filled rooms over a bunch of free-market radicals who called for major bloodletting. She was surprised, however, to hear an outcry about government overreach coming from the very guys who, just two years ago, came to Washington, hat in hand, and got a blank check, no questions asked. "I'd rather they just said 'thank you' and went on their way," she thought, channeling Col. Jessup.

This year, the panel discussion that Vika was solely interested in attending featured Gray Chancellor as a speaker. She did not expect to be let in on some secret trade, she just wanted to get a feel for what the big guys were up to. At this stage of her career, Vika knew that all good trades are never secret — they are there for all to see. What matters is if you put it on or not. Over the years, Vika had developed an ability to separate those who talk for a living from those who act, along with a simmering disdain for those who, while in a business of risk, never risk anything.

Gray Chancellor, like many Wall Street bigwigs who landed on their feet in the wake of the crisis by either opening their own hedge fund or jumping to a different shop, was now a member of senior management at a large American bank. For people like Gray Chancellor, there's no retirement because at some point their careers are not about money; at a certain point, it all becomes about the name, and the battles one wins.

Surviving the storm and landing a senior position at a prominent financial institution kept Gray Chancellor's name in the industry grapevine. Not that he was seeking publicity, but, after his former employer went bust and the government had to step in to arrange a quick rescue with the help of his former rival, it came with the territory. Many of his former comrades had been dodging investigators, and the press had a feeding frenzy dragging their names through the mud. Gray Chancellor hadn't been charged with any wrongdoing, but he became a frequent witness before endless Senate and House Banking Committee panels. Some amount of public remorse needed to be shown, he thought, to clear his name and the names of his firm and colleagues from shameless insinuations in the press. But, other than forced public appearances, he kept his head low and focused on the job. People like him were built for survival, not retreat.

The annual panel appearance in Miami had almost become an old habit, one of the indulgences he carried over from his former life. People still wanted to hear him speak and conference organizers always went out of their way to have him attend. The panels facilitated by traders and portfolio managers were the most entertaining — these were the true men of action. Gray Chancellor and a couple of other traders on the panel proceeded to describe, in down-to-earth terms, what the situation was, where one could find value and what to avoid. Veteran traders, the kind who had seen it all, had killed and been killed several times on trades in the course of their careers, developed their own no-nonsense manner of speech. Fancy words and terms are for analysts, newbies and investment bankers — those in the business of impressing a boss or a client.

Gray Chancellor wasn't trying to impress anyone; he was preoccupied with navigating the new terrain, holding his finger to the wind.

"What we are looking at these days is not the minutiae of a bond's performance. We are more concerned about the macro situation. We think the pertinent question these days is what Washington is doing. We are watching particularly closely the upcoming legislation related to foreclosures. You can pretty much throw away all those models that the math PhDs built for you over the years. We are in a new zeitgeist. Today, your P&L will depend on how the government treats foreclosures, and the Fed's monetary policy. This is uncharted territory. This kind of risk is not quantifiable: It's not a numbers problem anymore. It requires a sort of situational awareness. A few connections in D.C. would also help." Gray Chancellor's joke prompted some nervous laughter in the audience.

Gray Chancellor was aware of the natural human tendency to solve new problems with old tools, but hoped that his presentation had cleared up at least some of the misconceptions among the investment crowd. But the cast of old habits and routines proved to be too hard to break. The Q&A session that followed confirmed his assessment.

"Do you use OAS spread to determine the amount of hedge you put on?" someone in the audience asked.

OAS, or Option Adjusted Spread, was one of those fancy but increasingly useless measures that Gray Chancellor had warned against during his presentation. Surprised to hear that kind of question after everything he had just said, he proceeded to patiently enlighten the questioner. "We really don't rely on OAS like we did before, we just try to use the cash-flow methodology. But, like I mentioned earlier, we're more concerned about what the Fed and the Congress will do." He began steering the conversation to a more pertinent topic.

"But how do you measure the probability then? Do you use historical data?" someone else interrupted.

Gray Chancellor, mildly annoyed by such stubborn blindness, nonetheless smiled and said, "Well, that's the problem, isn't it? We don't because we can't. No one can today. How do you expect to measure a six-sigma event? Or an event that has no numerical value? Today, there are uncertainties that really can't be measured with the tools we have. But if you're looking for some sort of broad guidelines, just be concerned about the macro situation, not the product itself."

Another hand went up. "Do you think that Congress can pass legislation that will allow underwater homeowners to write off their principal?"

"That's a good question," he said, relieved to field an intelligent question. "Frankly, and this is my personal opinion, while we should be mindful of government actions, specifically the Fed, I don't see more downside to the industry coming from Congress. There's no way Congress can pass anything that will violate the sanctity of mortgage contracts. A business contract is the cornerstone of American democracy. So, those loans will most likely go into foreclosure, not into any sort of modification."

"What about HAMP[14] and HARP[15] and all those other government programs meant to help homeowners?"

"Well, I think those programs exist solely as a storefront. They were never meant to work on a big scale. While they may help a handful of people who qualify, this is not something that could negatively affect mortgage bonds in any significant way."

Some in the audience sighed with relief. Gray Chancellor quickly wrapped up the panel.

Vika, amused with the exchange, emailed back to the office: "There's still a lot of regulatory uncertainty, but some think it's all for show. Plus, there's a lot of dumb money sitting on the sidelines waiting to jump in. They have nowhere else to go." She paused for a moment, reminiscing on her first encounter with Gray Chancellor years ago, then put her Blackberry back in her purse and headed for the pool bar where she was supposed to meet Neal Bitterman.

***

Vika found Neal immersed in his Blackberry.

"Mind if I sit here?"

"Yeah, sure." Neal looked up and saw Vika standing

---

14   Home Affordable Modification Program.
15   Home Affordable Refinance Program.

next to him. "Oh, hey. What's going on, dude?"

"Not much. What's up with you?"

"Same ol', same ol'."

Vika sighed. "I need a drink."

"So, what are you up to?" Neal asked, signaling a bartender.

"Went to a few panels. It doesn't look good. Do you think the money will ever make its way to underwater homeowners? The big guys are saying that there's no mechanism for it. And all that talk that we hear, it's all just to placate the public."

"It all depends on how they decide to prioritize everything."

"No. Even if they decide to prioritize the homeowners, which is unlikely, they have no way of giving money directly to them other than writing down the principal. And how the hell are they going to do that? Abdicate the contracts? No one is going to vote for it, not in this Congress."

"Abrogate, not abdicate."

"Whatever, smartass." Vika gulped down her vodka-cranberry.

They both sat quiet for a while. The pool bar's TV screens, set to CNBC to accommodate the convention crowd, provided a distraction to the sudden lull in conversation. "Foreclosure-related suicides are on the rise," read the running headline at the bottom of the screen.

Neal snapped out of his contemplation. "Hey, when were you at Baruch Wolf?"

"Years ago. Why?"

"I just heard some guy who used to work there killed himself. Was unemployed for a long time. Couldn't get a job and couldn't pay his bills. Shot himself in his backyard."

"Oh my God! Do you know his name?"

"Don't remember. Kevin... Yeah, Kevin something."

"Oh no! I think I know the guy. I just saw him, like, a few months ago at a fundraiser. He was... he was looking for a job."

"Yeah. Tough. Wife and two kids. Apparently did it so they could collect life insurance."

"I can't believe it. If only I could help him then. But maybe... maybe pretty soon we won't even be able to help ourselves."

"Dude, let's not get gloomy. We just have to hold on some more and survive this. Just do your job, sit tight and this will all be over. Just be better than your teammates, do better research, find some value and you'll be fine."

"Better research? Research doesn't matter at all these days." She caught sight of the bartender, pointed at her drink and made the "another round" sign.

"Well, sure it does. For instance, I keep a spreadsheet just for myself of all the bonds that cross my desk: I know the size, who owns them, where they last traded and who has an axe for them so that, no matter where I go, I always have this little cache of ideas with me. You have to get your own competitive advantage." Neal began to sound like he was speaking to a child.

"How can you be so delusional? And let's assume that you do all that, that you hang on somehow because you're special. And you are special, with your Ivy League degree and your impressive resume and your stupid spreadsheet. But what about everyone else? You'll survive, but at what cost? What good is it to survive when none of your customers will? You'll have a seat and a desk, but what are you going to do? Do you really think all that money is going to make its way to people's pockets? Congress doesn't have the balls to write checks directly to households. Everyone is on his own now. There's no cavalry coming."

"And why do you care about them? They got what they deserve. They shouldn't have taken out loans they can't pay back."

Vika was now in a full debate mode. "They didn't just take the loans — somebody gave it to them. They'd be fools not to take free money. As a trader, you should know. And what do they know? They have a high school diploma and an American Dream. They've been told for decades that owning a house is the crux of human existence. How can we expect them to know what's going on? Who was going to let them know about the fine print?"

"I always knew you were a Commie, Vic. It's called personal responsibility and if they don't know what they get themselves into, they get what they deserve."

"I'm not a Commie. I love the game. I live for the game. But this is not a game anymore. This is carnage! People like us need those folks to do business, we need them at our table. Why do we have to destroy them? They have to be nurtured and protected and taken care of, you know, like players in the casino. But they got destroyed. We destroyed them. And now... now it's our turn."

"I didn't destroy them, their own stupidity did. And by

the way, I wasn't the one shorting the market. You were. I'm just a middleman."

"And you didn't expect people to be stupid, in their mass? You thought they were all rational and acted in their self-interest?"

"Sure. Because if they aren't, it's their fault and they suffer the consequences."

"But it's not them who suffer the consequences now. It's you! It's us! That equity piece has been wiped out and now the losses have reached us — the smart, the responsible, the rational." Vika was in a full-blown-rant mode and on to her third drink.

"And what do you suggest we do? Have Uncle Sam tell banks and lenders what they can and cannot do? Then we'll both be without jobs."

"Without jobs," Vika scoffed. "It's your biggest fear, isn't it? Can't you see? How can you not see it? We've all been played for suckers! We've been asked to work hard with the promise of a reward. But our reward was that we became addicts. We could have made a few hundred grand a year for the rest of our lives and been happy. But we wanted to make millions. Because we had a way to do it. But in the end we got shit. A year from now, no one will need us. And now Wall Street is your whole life. You're nothing without it. It consumed you. You're afraid to be who you are, afraid to even think certain thoughts, afraid to like certain things, lest the System," Vika mockingly bulged out her eyes, "gets wise and spits you out. We are robots. We are marching like those school kids in a Pink Floyd video. And yet, even if you comply, it will discard you like a used condom. How can you be loyal to such a machine? You're afraid to even think of yourself as not having a desk, not having a Bloomberg terminal, because without a Bloomberg, you're nothing. Your skills and your stupid little spreadsheet don't mean shit if you don't have a Bloomberg. And they count on our compliance because without them, without the platform, we're nobodies. They know we have nowhere to go. You'll do and say anything to keep your seat and a desk. Who are you without it? A nice guy? What else? What do you even like? Who are you?"

"I work hard. I pay my taxes. I pay my bills. I'm a model citizen."

"Bullshit! Work hard toward what? Helping small businesses raise cash? But that's not what we do. Toward paying your bills? But everyone does! Why does that make you special, because your bills are bigger? Why have such bills in the first place? Why set yourself up for a lifetime of servitude? And they know it. They know! They know you'll crawl on broken glass to have a chair and a desk. They expect you to defend what they're doing. Anything but to be in free fall, anything but to be yourself. This is your biggest fear — to be yourself."

"Dude, what are you saying? Who are *they*? You're drunk and you don't know what you're talking about. Stop embarrassing yourself, people are staring at you. I think we should call it a night."

Vika, drunk and agitated, continued. "I'm not drunk and you're just scared. You're scared!"

Neal, grim-faced, picked up the bill. "Come on, I'll walk you to your room."

"Oh, great. Maybe I'll get lucky."

"I doubt it."

***

After Vika came back from the conference, she struggled to get back to her normal routine. She spent her days sitting at her desk in stupor, staring lethargically at her screens. Her usual self-rationalizations that she had employed with decreasing effect over the past few years had now collapsed. Her standard motivations that had kept her afloat before — the virtues of hard work, her hard-won access to the front-desk position, the lifestyle she'd gotten used to, her aspirations of a benevolent future — failed to placate her now.

"Why continue doing this?" she thought. "To what end? What's the best-case scenario that I'm working toward? Friday nights at the opera, summers in France, winters in the Caribbean? And then what? I can't just retire and sit on the beach with a mojito and do nothing. I'll go nuts after two weeks. Or am I looking to make a few bucks and become a nice person, active in the New York charity circle? What a nauseating, sickening prospect. I would have to become one of those polished, empty phonies at charity balls, drinks in hand, smiling for cameras, pretending to care. But how can I keep pretending? The game is rigged and, despite my decade-long illusions, I'm not the one doing the rigging. If I leave the game, I would be negating my own self. But to stay… to stay I'd have to acquiesce, to accept my depravity and never revisit it again. I'd have to *let them win*."

Dispirited, but with her mind made up, Vika purposely showed slack in her daily routines. Slacking required some effort. Because of the rigid discipline she'd developed over a decade, being punctual and industrious had become second nature. Before, she would arrive at her desk by 7:30 a.m. and leave only after Lee left. Now, although she still woke up at 6 a.m., she sat around the apartment, numb, mindlessly watching CNBC, and struggled against the urge to head out the door and show up at work before 9 a.m. During the afternoons, she would disappear from her desk to spend more than an hour at the gym and then ended her workday at 5 p.m. sharp, even while Lee was still sitting at his desk — an unspeakable display of insolence and insubordination. Lee got the message pretty quickly and, after a week of such mutiny, called her into his office.

"So, Vika, tell me, why should I keep you here?"

"You have no reason to do so. You should just let me go."

Lee, expecting some sort of self-defense, was surprised. "You want to leave?"

"Yeah. I can't do this anymore. It's hard to explain. I'm drained of all of my resources. I feel expended, squeezed like a lemon. One more day of this and I'll go nuts. I need to go away for at least six months to take my mind off things. I can't be useful on the desk right now."

Lee took a pause. "You realize that after you get back you will not have a seat and a desk. You'll be going nowhere in this market. I just want you to be aware of the full repercussions of this move."

"I am aware."

"Well, you have two weeks of vacation left. Why don't you go away and think it over? And then we'll talk about this when you come back."

"Thank you, Lee, but I doubt I'll change my mind."

"Well, if you are determined to leave then I can probably arrange a package for you. They're doing another round of redundancies here, so we can just make you redundant. That way you can keep your benefits for a few months."

"Thank you. That would be nice."

"You sure that's what you want to do?"

"Yes, I'm absolutely positive. I liked working for you, but I can't be a part of it anymore. I just don't like *this* game. And I know I'll probably be a bum for a while, but I can't stay on the desk anymore. Sorry, Lee, nothing personal."

"Well, I will be sorry to see you go. But frankly, I don't think any of us will be here for much longer. So, who knows, maybe you're making a good move. Still, take the two weeks off and think it over. It's a serious decision."

"Sure."

Chapter
7

WALL STREET EXECUTIVES' TESTIMONIES ON Capitol Hill, a ritualistic public exorcism, became a staple of daytime business TV in the years after the collapse. A peculiar act became routine: A tarnished Wall Street titan would come in, deliver a choreographed statement, show some remorse, mix in some face-saving defiance where appropriate, promise it would "never happen again," and go back to his business.

Such public catharsis was a great tactical move for both sides. Politicians got to exhibit, consequence-free, their independent streak by wagging their fingers and chastising their major political contributors, and grim-faced and heavily counseled Wall Street execs got a chance to feign humility and play along.

Gray Chancellor was again scheduled to testify alongside

a few other banking officials, now as a high-profile executive of a large American bank. By now, he had gotten used to the occasional public self-flagellation. He understood that this was just part of the game. It was just something that needed to be done, given the circumstances.

Many invitees were careful not to piss off Warren Banks, an aggressive Democratic congressman on the Financial Services Committee and Wall Street's biggest foe. But other than that old crank Banks, who had a penchant for long and damning diatribes against Wall Street executives, the committee members were rather harmless: They either didn't know enough to mount any sort of attack or, if they did, had to choose their words carefully so as not to damage their relationships with their major political donors.

Virgil Chambault, a Republican congressman from South Carolina — fresh from winning a tactical fight against Democrats over the U.S. budget — was in a jolly mood. He had led the insurgency of his fellow deficit hawks in Congress by devising a simple, foolproof plan: They would refuse to honor U.S. debt obligations, essentially allowing the U.S. to default on its debt, unless Democrats agreed to cut spending. These drastic measures were warranted, in his view, by the gravity of the status quo. Some bloodletting was justified to "keep this great country of ours from slipping into socialism," he claimed. The standoff worked brilliantly. Markets nosedived and Democrats had no choice but to comply. Moreover, the move helped burnish his small-government and business-friendly credentials — surely business leaders must hate the deficit as much as he does. He viewed his role on the Committee as representing those business interests and considered any attempts at regulatory activity to be a detriment to economic growth.

Gray Chancellor began with prepared remarks.

GRAY CHANCELLOR: Chairman Chambault, Ranking Member Banks, and Members of the Committee. I come here today to discuss recent regulatory changes that will affect the financial services industry in general and my firm in particular. All of our clients, big and small, rely on our services on a daily basis and we have been a reliable market player for decades. As a global institution, we continue to strive to provide the best services to our clients, to attract and nurture the best talent, and to increase value for our shareholders.

Thus, I am disappointed that, despite our best efforts, we have suffered some lapses in our risk management. Granted, some of our employees, our senior management and I, personally, failed to apply the required level of scrutiny to some of our positions. We failed to give appropriate weight to some of our riskier assets and we failed to anticipate how it might affect our risk ratios during the recent market turmoil. Our reputation took a long time to build, and I fully intend to repair it and restore our good standing in the community. I will personally see that we are in compliance with new rules and regulations. No one is more invested in the success of our organization, our customers, and our employees than I am.

We are making significant progress. In

anticipation of the new capital requirements, we instructed our risk-management unit to reduce both our exposure in risk-weighted assets and in the corresponding risk. We're rebuilding our capital base by getting rid of bad assets, by issuing new stock and by reducing leverage. We fully cooperate with regulators and we're applying our best judgment to evaluate the risk in our portfolios, to minimize our exposure and to position ourselves to withstand possible market dislocations without damage to our investors and taxpayers. There's not an area of the balance sheet that has gone unchecked.

Despite setbacks, we intend to remain competitive on the global scale and to continue to provide first-class service to all our clients. We are a dedicated group of skilled and experienced professionals who care about the future direction of the firm. We acknowledged our mistakes, took action and are now ready to move forward. I am convinced that together we can learn from the experience and put this chapter behind us. I pledge my commitment to transparency and I'm prepared to answer any questions coming from the public or public officials. Thank you, and I'm now ready to take your questions.

REP. WARREN BANKS (D-MA): Thank you for agreeing to meet with us here today. We've seen some progress on the regulatory front, but we're far from safe ground. There are still many areas that require special attention and, as evidenced by recent lapses in your risk-management unit, there's still a lot of work to be done. Let's say you're the brightest crayon in the box, you're fully aware of the workings of your organization and you keep an eye on all kinds of positions that would otherwise get out of control. Let's give you the benefit of the doubt. Now, wouldn't it be right to ask what will happen after you're gone? What if your successor is not as bright, not as well-informed, not as disciplined? Are we, as citizens, just supposed to hold our collective breath and keep our fingers crossed every time a large financial institution changes its management? Are we solely dependent on the personal assurances of the next guy?

GRAY CHANCELLOR: Congressman, let me begin by saying that there are multiple levels of control in place right now. We are complying with new regulations, we're raising regulatory capital, we're meeting new standards. Many capable and experienced people are in charge, and all the bad apples have been let go. The system is cleansing itself as we speak. And trust me, neither I nor anyone in our management want to be in that kind of spotlight again.

REP. BANKS: But you can't really say that capable and experienced people weren't in charge before. Today you do want things to quiet down and you want everyone off your back. But when all is forgotten, let's say ten years from now, things will go back to usual, someone else will be in charge, someone less introspective and more ambitious than you. Shouldn't we institute some controls against so much power in so few hands? Would, for instance, breaking banks into smaller parts help? No matter how smart you are, you can't possibly know what's happening in all the units of such a sprawling business.

GRAY CHANCELLOR: Breaking up our bank into smaller parts would severely undermine our competitiveness against the European banks. We're already hampered by the new capital requirements, and reducing our size even further would rob us of the market share. We would have to lay off more people. Our stock would collapse. While I understand and appreciate your concerns, and I do want to help and I have been in compliance with new rules, my main loyalty is to my shareholders and clients. At the end of the day, we're a business, not a non-profit.

REP. BANKS: OK, let's move on. You said that you wanted in particular to have smart regulations as opposed to more regulations. The CFTC[16] budget was $200 million for the year, but the Appropriations Committee just voted not to give it any additional funds. Do you think that at that level we can get smart regulations out of CFTC?

GRAY CHANCELLOR: I have never looked at CFTC budgets. I don't know what they need. It's almost impossible for me to comment on it.

REP. BANKS: I'm surprised, because it does seem to me that you are well-informed about the aspects

---

16   Commodity Futures Trading Commission, an agency that regulates futures and options markets.

of what the federal government does and doesn't do. And to talk about smart regulations, but in effect give them a pass on a substantial budget reduction, well… But that's your answer. Next question. You say that your institution is financially sound, but what about other banks that are in worse shape and have weaker balance sheets? Is there a danger that those kinds of institutions might cause some problems?

GRAY CHANCELLOR: I don't know. But I think we should all take comfort in the fact that all American banks are better capitalized. The system is far stronger today–

REP. BANKS: I appreciate it, but it wasn't the question I asked. We can't assume that it's going to be this way forever. There are some who are resisting the recapitalization. What about others who are not as special and not as savvy as you?

GRAY CHANCELLOR: I can't speak for others.

Representative Virgil Chambault (R–SC): I'd like to cut in, Congressman Banks–

REP. BANKS: And how can we be sure that your best judgment is really the best way–

REP. CHAMBAULT: Your time is up. I request the microphone, Congressman, if you please.

REP. BANKS: OK, I yield to the Congressman from South Carolina.

REP. CHAMBAULT: Thank you. I really appreciate you for coming here today and talking to us. It is important that we talk about things happening in the industry, and to have you advise us and help, I think, as we look forward to finding the best-practice scenarios for the industry. In Washington, we, too, lose money every day. [Chambault snickers at his own wit.] So, the intent here today is really not to sit in judgment but to understand what happened.

I'd like to start by asking, what do you consider smart regulations? What advice would you give to lawmakers? I'm asking you about the recent regulatory bill that a lot of us here are frustrated about and a lot of bank managers, I think, too. And as I've mentioned, perhaps, we're not capable of doing it right. But I would like to come out of the hearing today with some ideas. What do you think we need to do to, uh, allow the industry to operate better. I'm really honestly looking for some ideas as we look over the next year and hopefully be in a position where we can make some positive change.

GRAY CHANCELLOR: I... um...

REP. CHAMBAULT: Do you think that the new financial regulations made our banking system safer? And if you were to write financial legislation, what would you write?

GRAY CHANCELLOR: I, um, we supported the-

REP. CHAMBAULT: I know what you supported, but has it made our financial system safer? I'm talking about the regulatory regime that Congress put in place.

"You've gotta be kidding me," Gray Chancellor thought to himself. "What the fuck does he want me to say about it? Doesn't he realize we have lobbyists precisely for that sort of discussion?"

```
GRAY CHANCELLOR: Congressman, writing legisla-
tion is not my business. I'm not sure I can answer
your question.
```

Gray Chancellor was well aware of the political dynamics in Congress. Except for that old crank Banks, both Democrats and Republicans were receiving money from his firm. Both were critical of "Wall Street" when back in their home districts. That unnerved him. But, unlike many of his colleagues on the Street, Gray Chancellor understood the game and played along. "These guys have to get tough on us in public," he thought. "It's just part of their job, given the circumstances. But what the hell is this guy doing?"

```
REP. CHAMBAULT: Do you think we need regula-
tions at all? Do you think regulations impede firms
like yours from being competitive, the way things
stand right now?
```

A lot was going through Gray Chancellor's mind at this point. He came there armed with dodges, with esoteric terms he was prepared to throw at politicians if things got heated, letting them know that they didn't know shit. What he didn't expect was such an ingratiating attitude. He experienced sheer disbelief, bemusement mixed with the breathtaking realization that these were the schmucks who were supposed to police someone like him, that these douchebags were the only thing standing between guys like him and the average Joe, that he and guys like him were the sole de-facto arbiters of a system that affects millions of people and billions of dollars.

Gray Chancellor deplored the Democrats for their constant attempts to vilify him. But, even though a registered Republican himself, he despised the current Republican majority even more for their intractable obstruction when it came to simple fiscal matters, for their ideological zeal and their determination to score points in the business community so obsessively that, with their scorched-earth approach, they nearly cost the economy hundreds of billions last summer. These self-proclaimed business-friendly guys were bad for business.

"My own D.C. liaisons tried to reason with him, tried to bring some sense into him, begged him to back off, but to no avail," Gray Chancellor thought. "And now this motherfucker is trying to be friends with me?" Such crude play aggravated him even more than those who displayed open hostility toward him. "What is this fool trying to do here? Is he trying to secure a lobbying job for himself? What does he expect me to say here, now, after I've done years of public contrition and remorse, after we've spent millions complying with their stupid regulations?"

GRAY CHANCELLOR: I appreciate your trust in my expertise, Congressman. As I said, I'm not against regulations, not in a way you want me to be. But let's be mindful of what we're trying to accomplish. For some reason you're pushing me to go full John Galt here, but doing so would make both of our pictures appear on the front pages tomorrow. I don't seek publicity, and I don't want my name to be sliced and diced in tomorrow's papers. I have been a punching bag for politicians and for everyone else long enough. I don't want angry crowds with signs and pitchforks standing near my office. I'm here today to simply answer your questions about my business, not to promote your ideology.

Suppressed gasps echoed through the suddenly quiet room. Virgil Chambault, instantly somber, made another attempt to steer the conversation.

REP. CHAMBAULT: I am gauging whether your business would be better served by having some industry experts weigh in on the state of affairs. I am trying to assess how regulatory uncertainty could hamper your operations.

This was about as much sycophancy as Gray Chancellor could take.

GRAY CHANCELLOR: Uncertainty? I'm glad you brought that up. You know, if it wasn't for this Congress's thoughtless and, dare I say, juvenile brinkmanship a few months back, when you decided to play with our country's credit rating and brought us all to the verge of default just to indulge your utopian worldview, we wouldn't even be talking about this. The danger to the financial system is no longer coming from whether guys like me follow your rules. It's coming from your own kindergarten ideas about how the economy works, and from your thoughtless actions. Frankly, we in the business community don't know what to expect from you anymore. Your methods are unsound, Congressman. Your entire caucus has got off the boat. You split from the entire… program. And you have the nerve to talk about uncertainty?

REP. CHAMBAULT: What boat? What program?

GRAY CHANCELLOR: It's a metaphor, Congressman. Never mind.

REP. CHAMBAULT: Let me remind you that you are testifying before the United States Congress and that you're under oath. Perhaps this isn't the time to be witty.

GRAY CHANCELLOR: I was just illustrating a point. But let's get back to regulations. Whatever regulations are eventually written will not adequately address whatever business is doing at that point. Regulations are always one step behind. Let's be mindful of that. I'm not the one to help you figure out what to do about that, it is simply not my job. I do my thing, you do your thing. If I tell you what I really think needs to be done, it will go beyond whatever ideology or piece of legislation you pin all your hopes on. The real kind of reform would require all of you, Congressmen, from different sides of the aisle to get on the same page; it would require getting the Fed and U.S. regulators in the same room with the Bank of England and the Europeans. We all know it's never going to happen, not after what you just pulled off.

And while I sympathize with your desire to secure your place in history, I can't help you with that. I'm not in the business of saving the world, but I'm good at what I do. Are you good at what you do, Congressman? I spent years doing public apology tours and trying to bring everybody at my firm to comply with your new regulations. I did that, and that's what I'm here to talk about today. And then I just want to go back to my business. So, if you want to talk about regulations, let's talk about regulations. But really, there's no need for you to expose yourself like this.

Silence in the room was only interrupted by the fast clicking of cameras. Reporters couldn't have asked for a better development. Journalists and bloggers got busy with snarky editorials. Twitter lit up. Traders watching the entire exchange on their CNBC screens cheered and hollered. And the public went about their business.

***

FOR IMMEDIATE RELEASE

South Carolina Congressman Virgil Chambault, a conservative Republican who rose to prominence as the leader of the Tea Party caucus, announces his resignation from Congress.

He will join the American Legacy Foundation, a conservative business lobbying group, as President.

"I'm leaving the Congress, but I'm not leaving the fight," Mr. Chambault said in a statement. "I've decided that my skills and resources will be better applied outside the Beltway gridlock. The conservative movement needs new leadership and active engagement in the battle of ideas. We can't keep compromising ourselves into irrelevance. The American public deserves conservatives who are unafraid to stand for their principles and who will keep this country from slipping further into socialism."

Chapter

8

WALL STREET DOES NOT RELEASE its disciples cost-free.
First, it makes sure they're mental and emotional
cripples, and then lets them decide if they still want to leave.
Wall Street refugees' mental capacities have atrophied to the
point where they've lost the ability to function in the outside
world. "Back to the coalmine!" their tortured minds, ill-
equipped to deal with large amounts of free time, implore.
Seeking action, they're ready to occupy themselves with the
next pursuit, but they forgot what they like. What good is
freedom if you don't know what to do with it? What if those
decades spent on nurturing discipline, worshipping busyness, and methodically ridding themselves of leisure prevent
them from shaking off that character overnight and becoming carefree hobos? Like prisoners released after twenty years
behind bars, they're so used to the routine and the rules that

the lack of structure is debilitating.

Vika spent her afternoons dazed, wandering around Greenwich Village, catching a matinee at Angelica Film Center and hanging around Strand bookstore. She wasn't buying anything, she just spent hours skimming through classic and contemporary authors, bewildered by what she'd missed over the years. She realized she hadn't read a book — a real book, not industry research — in more than a decade. "How do you even begin to fill such a void?" she pondered.

Vika didn't have any coherent plans for the future. Such a state of affairs embarrassed her. Before, she'd always had a plan, and now, at a time when her peers were settling into life routines that would carry them all the way into retirement, she was abandoning ship.

Shell-shocked, she found an outlet in the local poker scene.

A poker table is a distilled Darwinian preserve. It's a modern-day Wild West, where a hand can either strike gold or deteriorate into an OK Corral shootout. "The gunfight is in the head, not in the hands," a gunslinger once said, and he was right. In the long run, the best mind wins, not the hands that have been dealt.

Poker awards us a luxurious clarity. It spares us from misjudging others' intentions. Everyone at the table has the sole goal of taking our stack. This simple axiom is liberating. It invites us to check our hubris and identity at the door and focus on the game; whether we decide to accept the invitation is up to us. In realm of poker, there are no men, women, straights, gays, Republicans, Democrats, religious, atheists. It's a free-membership club with no agenda and no tolerance for illusions, biases or morality tales — just the rules, ordained and enforced by the Poker Gods.

The rules are strict but simple: Poker asks, nay, commands all its adherents to cut the bullshit and embrace reality. It will toy with the deluded — those who have everything figured out — with the playful cruelty of a cat toying with a mouse. Bring all of your convictions and credentials, your anger and insecurities to the poker table and the Poker Gods will tease you and mock you and fill you with false hopes and send you to the ATM a few times before releasing you, broke and steaming, at 5am.

Vika knew this, and not just by observation. She, too, often went down in flames with an "I have Kings, motherfucker!" war cry. She pursued the elusive *correct* play religiously, but suspected that the chip on her shoulder and her lack of patience prevented her from being a good player.

This self-awareness came in handy, however, when polished and smug Wall Street types played at her table. She knew how they thought — they treated every hand as if their manhood was at stake. They are smart, they are used to scouting value, used to winning, and thus have a reasonable expectation to crush the philistines. That's what they do at their day job. But the Poker Gods are not suckers, they don't care about one's real-life titles and arrangements. Here at the poker table, the lonely redoubt of an unrigged game, the philistines and the unwashed will scoop a Managing Director's stack with the audacity and indifference of a bear devouring a neglectful tourist's lunch.

The unwashed rubes consumed Vika's attention. The poorly dressed, quiet, often smelly disciples of the game happened to be the best players. The only image they cared about was the size of the stack in front of them. Those uncouth wizards live only for the game, for the win! Vika envied that kind of mental prowess.

New York offered a variety of underground poker clubs, and every night there was a game going on somewhere in the city. One night, at a seedy Garment District loft conveniently tucked away between a rub-and-tug upstairs and a Chinese restaurant downstairs, Vika lost a nice pot with the top two pair to a scummy-looking, fat, middle-aged guy in a hoodie. He caught an unlikely gutshot draw on the river to make a straight.

"What?! 5-7 offsuit?" Vika was incredulous to see his hand at the showdown.

"Too many callers, I had the odds."

"Odds?! What odds? You had freaking 8 percent on the turn!" she hissed, even more aggravated.

"Implied odds. I figured you were gonna put your entire stack in there with your two pair."

"You got lucky this time. Whatever. Nice hand, sir." Vika was annoyed, but forced herself to be a good sport.

"Hey, you wanna go to a Rush concert this week?" he said in return, peeking from behind his mountain of chips. "I'll take you backstage, I have passes."

"You asking me out?!" Vika squeaked, incredulous, looking around the table to share her glee with others. But everyone was too immersed in the game to pay attention.

"Asking you out? I'm not suicidal. You look like you'll assault me if I say something wrong," the guy shot back.

"I do?" Vika tried to assume an indignant tone, but couldn't hold back the chuckle. "I do, don't I? Dude, I appreciate it, but a Rush concert is kinda lame. It's probably full of…" Vika was about to list a hundred reasons why a Rush concert would suck.

"Suit yourself," the guy snipped.

Vika looked down at the now-empty felt in front of her, contemplating his offer. "A rock concert is not such a bad idea," she thought. "If the guy is a maniac or a boor, at least I can deal with it at the concert. Besides, what if he's not full of it? What's the downside?"

She looked back up and asked, "How did you get backstage passes?"

"I know Geddy Lee."

"Who's Geddy Lee?"

"The lead singer. You know, the one with high voice."

"How do you know him?"

"It's a long story."

Not a big Rush fan, Vika was nonetheless intrigued. She'd never been backstage at a rock concert.

"OK, I'll think about it," Vika said. "Are you, by any chance, friends with Robert Plant?"

"Unfortunately, no. Only Geddy Lee. And you don't have much time to think — the concert is this Friday and I have plenty of friends who are lining up for that pass. So, you want it or not?"

Accustomed to quick decision-making, Vika figured that the upside outweighed the downside. "Sure, I'll go. If you're not full of it."

***

Though a mere toddler in the '70s, Vika was a connoisseur of that glorious and troubled decade — the music, the clothes, the drugs! She had seen her share of aging rock bands. Although many of those bands had, in her opinion, turned into caricatures of their former selves, she still wanted to catch a glimpse of that long-gone era before they bit the dust forever. Each one of those previous concerts attracted about an equal number of men and women. But a Rush concert is different. A Rush concert is a sausage fest. It's a white-libertarian-male jamboree. Perhaps it has something to do with the lyrics. Listening to Rush actually requires knowing and appreciating their convoluted lyrics. Combine this with some melodies that are hard to hum along with, and you have a formula repellent to most women. In Rush songs, there's no room for mysticism, heartbreak, desire, sex or riot — themes that touch people on a primeval level. Rush celebrates cerebral over visceral. It is all about reason and logic and personal choice.

Madison Square Garden was a place to behold. The crowd was orgasmic. The concert brought together middle-aged dads with their teenage sons, whom they hoped to wean off hip-hop and introduce to real music; dorky, pale-faced twentysomethings abandoning their cyber lives for a brief real-life experience; longhaired, balding drifters; and a few haughty Wall Street suits with clients occupying the best seats near the stage. Many in the room were singing along, unfazed by the complex progressive-rock melodies and brainy lyrics, demonstrating a serious allegiance to the band. This gathering — the recitation of words, the knowing glances between strangers, the rapturous expressions on every fan's face — was akin to witnessing a religious pilgrim-age.

The band played their '70s hits, shunning their newer stuff to the audience's delight. After the show, Vika and her poker buddy separated from the crowds and made their way into the backstage lounge where snacks and drinks were already awaiting the lucky few. Among them, Vika spotted a few comedic actors whose names she didn't remember.

After meeting Geddy Lee and taking a mandatory Facebook-bound picture with him, Vika went to the bathroom. Yellow maintenance tape blocked the men's bathroom door, an unthinkable management oversight at a Rush concert, where the men-to-women ratio exceeds ten to one. She grinned and proceeded to her designated lavatory, which was operational and, for the time being, coed. All the stalls were empty except for one.

"Good thing I only need to pee," thought Vika with relief. "God forbid there's some actor or a band member in there and I have a loud incident!"

Vika and the mysterious occupant exited their stalls simultaneously, exchanged understanding nods and smirks, and proceeded to the row of sinks and mirrors. The male stranger carried a whiff of self-assurance about him, the kind possessed only by people who always get what they want; there was no hint of doubt in his movements. He wore a typical Wall Street after-hours outfit: Pants and a business shirt, a sleeveless fleece vest with the KPMG logo on it meant to trick the lay observer into mistaking him for a mere accountant, and a low-slung baseball cap with the Guggenheim Capital logo. Wall Street power brokers, when looking to blend in with the crowd or stepping outside for a drink, are known to wear clothing with silly logos they have picked up at some conference as a diversion tactic. Such a contrived attempt at anonymity, combined with his location backstage at a freaking Rush concert, signaled that he was some kind of bigwig. Vika looked up sideways at his mirror. Gray Chancellor stared back at her, smiling. Vika gasped but continued to wash her hands in silence.

"So, how did you like the concert?" Gray Chancellor broke the silence.

"It's pretty awesome," Vika replied.

"Did you meet Geddy?"

"Yeah, I got a picture too."

"Which song did you like best?" he continued to chat, confident in the integrity of his anonymity.

"Freewill."

"Freewill? It's one of my favorites." He paused. "It's what separates the chaff from the wheat," he added to his reflection and, without expecting a reply, headed for the door.

In a split second, Vika lost her apprehensions. Here's the man who runs this whole freaking place, wallowing in his own delusions. She had to say something, now or never.

"I saw your testimony the other day," she blurted out.

Gray Chancellor stopped, processing what the girl had just said, then turned around to face Vika. His posture and voice projected the unfazed aura of a person accustomed to being surrounded, for years, by yes-men. "Oh, really? What did you think?"

"I thought that... I thought you were one of the few

people in the room who had a pretty clear idea about what's going on."

"I'm glad that's the impression you got. Do you know what's going on?"

"Yeah. I think you have been dealt a great hand, but you're playing it like a, like a, uh… you're not playing it correctly."

"Oh? How's that?"

"You are reacting to the events around you. You duck and cover where there's no imminent threat."

"Interesting. Go on."

"You're bulletproof and you know that. Regulators are either too dumb or too underfunded. Your lobbyists are pretty much writing the new laws. The public is outraged, but they can't really do anything either. Politicians pump their chests in public, but we know they're either on your payroll or have gone off the deep end. So, you are golden. But you act so defiant, as if regulations are going to harm you in some way."

"If you saw my testimony, you would know that I'm not against regulations."

"Well, you publicly accept them while trying to undermine them at every turn. And that is why neither the press nor the public will leave you alone. Like I said, you're not playing it correctly."

"OK. Let's hear your suggestion of a correct play." He crossed his arms and leaned against a sink with an intrigued look on his face.

"Embrace full reform and be vocal about it. It's a great

trade. Think about it: It has a limited downside and a big upside. If it fails, you go back to your business and say, 'Hey, guys, I tried. Now piss off.' And if it works, you will be a hero."

"Ha. If only things were that simple. I can't jeopardize thousands of employees and shareholders by sticking my neck out. And if the Europeans don't simultaneously do the same, then reform is a useless exercise. I don't want us to be at a disadvantage. It's just not something anyone can do at will, single-handedly. I can't act outside the framework."

"But you are the framework!"

"I'm just somebody who's simply doing his job."

"If you are just doing your job, then who is going to do what needs to be done?"

"What needs to be done?"

"Someone has to take care of the customers. What is it that you're pursuing at this point? Another billion-dollar deal? Philanthropy? Public office? I don't think any of the above make you get up in the morning. You could have retired a long time ago if you wanted to, but you're staying for something."

"I'm staying because someone has to do the job. Somebody has to run things and if I don't do it, someone else will. I have obligations to shareholders, to clients. There are factors you're not considering. What good would it be if I'm the only one pushing for changes? Unexpected moves from management would trigger an immediate stock sell-off and the board would not be pleased. No one knows this business as well as I do, but they would be forced to let me go. I'd be gone in an instant. Any sudden action would snowball out of proportion."

"That's how you explain it to yourself. But I think you're staying for the game. The thought of doing nothing scares you the most."

Gray Chancellor sneered. "You seem to assume a lot."

"I made a calculated guess."

"Are you a poker player?"

"I am."

"Good for you. But let me ask you this: Would you ever hesitate to take a fool's last stack? Especially if you knew that someone else is going to make a move for it? If you're really good at your game, you would make a move for his stack without a second thought."

"You're right, I would. But—"

"Then it's disingenuous of you to expect me to walk away or to change the rules."

"But we are not at a poker table, the fool can't stand up and leave if he doesn't like the game."

"No one can, but what we can do is to try to become better players. And I'm sure a smart girl like yourself will do just fine."

"I will. But the rubes! What about the rubes? Who's going to protect the rubes? When is the time for mercy?" Vika, collected up to this point, let out an earnest wail.

"The rubes, well… If someone chooses to be stupid, there's nothing I can do about it."

"No one chooses to be stupid. Maybe they just don't want to compete. Maybe we should just let the fools keep their last stack. Just for once."

"Look, I'm sorry for being the one to tell you there's no Santa, but…"

"Then we truly have no recourse. You are on some quest to show all of us how good you are at what you do. And we're all just dragged along for the ride."

Vika fell quiet.

Gray Chancellor used this pause to wrap things up. "Anyway, thank you for a delightful chat, but I gotta go. What's your name, by the way?"

"Vika."

"Nice talking to you, Vika. But I really gotta run. Someone has to take care of the rubes!" he said with a wink. "And good luck with your game," he added and walked out.

Epilogue

How can one be good if the framework doesn't allow it? Even more depressing: You can't call an architect and complain. And who is the architect anyway?

What a cruel joke it is, a tragic oversight, a great folly that Wall Street, omnipotent and illustrious, does not facilitate one with a shot at that glamorous slo-mo forward charge for the goal line, ball in hand, sweaty, scarred and victorious. What a shame that there can be no climactic Hollywood ending, no feel-good spectacular moment of splendor that the grateful public could watch and cheer and then create legends. How cool it would be if the Wall Street trading desks — a ragtag team of unsung, brilliant underdogs — had some powerful Dark Overlord to take on and defeat with the theme from *Rocky* playing in the background! What a glaring injustice it is that such promising potential of all those super-fit, aggressive and competitive overachievers, the best and the brightest, destined for great things, should be wasted on spreadsheets and pitch books and numbing all-nighters and legalistic choreography. After all, they were built for combat, for a valiant quest.

But there's no physical beauty in trading, no captivating, crowd-pleasing momentum. Alas, trading desks, where military and sports metaphors abound, are disappointingly poor venues for noble activities. There are no brothers-in-arms on the trading floor watching one another's backs under fire, no teammates hurling Hail Marys; only a bunch of witty bores quoting movie lines. And after you run all the marathons and bench-press all the weights in the company gym, what's there left to do? And who is there to save, and from whom? What if that moment for glory never comes? How sad and mundane this all is.

The illusion sets in: We're all here due to forces beyond our control, so we can be excused to wallow in indolence. Is there anything we do because we want to do it? Why, yes. If we can't be good, we can at least make sure we *feel* good. There *is* a time for introspection; we are not monsters, after all, just people doing their jobs. We provide liquidity, allocate capital, donate to charity. We must've done somebody some good.

And yet, we feel helpless.

Helpless we are no longer capable of being serious. Being serious is laughable. Snark is our defense against our impotence, our stupor. Faced with the profound, we hide behind witty and deflecting repartees. Serious actions or thoughts or intentions have to be veiled in nonchalance or avoided altogether, lest the people think that we are on some kind of mission.

And there's no release. The realm of Wall Street is not something you can switch off overnight or put on hold over the weekend or abandon when you quit. Once there, it's imprinted in your DNA, it becomes part of you, ingrained in your flesh. Like ex-military, restless and wistful in quiet suburbia, a Wall Street mind is entrapped, wishing for a battle, for action. Action, however contrived, is the only manifestation of its existence. So, you double your efforts and plow through and keep searching for that next big trade, stuck in a perpetual sprint for relevance, squeezed between the reality and the illusion.

I guess, that's when it's tough.